HOW TO BE A LIONESS

(NOT A PANDA)

FIND YOUR ROAR WITH THE WOMEN OF *TED LASSO*

BY LUCY BROADBENT

Uncommon Publishing

Disclaimer

This publication has not been prepared, approved, licensed, or authorized by the creators or producers of *Ted Lasso*, Warner Bros. Entertainment Inc., Apple TV+ or any entity involved in creating or producing the well-known TV show *Ted Lasso*.

The material in this publication is of the nature of general comment only. The advice and strategies contained herein may not be suitable for every situation. Readers should obtain professional advice and services where appropriate, particularly in the arena of mental health. Neither the publisher nor author shall be liable for damages arising. Any individuals, organizations or websites referred to in this work are citations and listed as potential sources for further information. Readers should be aware that websites listed in this work may change or disappear between the time of writing and when it is read.

CONTENTS

INTRODUCTION

"WHAT WOULD YOU rather be: a panda or a lion?" Keeley Jones is in the parking lot outside AFC Richmond asking her new friend Ted Lasso the question when Rebecca Welton, the club owner, overhears as she walks past. The answer is a lion, she calls over her shoulder. "Pandas are fat and lazy and have piss-stained fur. Lions are powerful and majestic and rule the jungle."

Tall, commanding, and with a halo of platinum blond hair, there is no escaping Rebecca's lioness qualities. If she let out a roar, it wouldn't surprise us. "What's black and white and red all over?" she demands, standing firm in her oh-so-high heels.

What? "A panda that gets anywhere near a f****** lion."

And so it begins, not just one of the most fabulous female friendships in recent TV history, but a flag being raised for women everywhere. Because, wishing no disrespect to pandas, who among us wouldn't want to be a strong, powerful ruler of the jungle? Or at least have the opportunity to choose to be if we wanted?

Lionesses—because we are talking about the girls here—also happen to be fast, strong, nimble, and most crucially, offer a support system for each other inside their pride. They hunt as a team. They do childcare as a team. They are fantastic examples of what happens when the girls look out for each other and work together.

When Hannah Waddingham and Juno Temple, the actors who play Rebecca Welton and Keeley Jones, respectively, met for the first time, it was in the restroom at the inaugural read-through of the *Ted Lasso* pilot script. They were about to play the only two female leads in a show packed full of men. Their immediate expectation was that their characters were likely to be pitted against each other in some competitive way. Female rivalry is a recurring theme in TV and film. Hollywood loves a catfight.

But the reality turns out to be the opposite, as anyone who has watched *Ted Lasso,* the Emmy award-winning Apple TV+ show, knows. The two women do not clash or fight. Instead, they become best friends and bring out the best in each other. Rebecca helps Keeley see that she is smarter than she gives herself credit for; Keeley helps Rebecca see that she is much more than a hurt, abandoned divorcée. Their friendship even blossoms into a business sponsorship when Rebecca offers Keeley a job, a moment so unusual in a comedy that it won the show praise not only from entertainment critics but also from women in business, lauding it as a mentorship role model.

And that is what this book is about. Just as self-improvement lessons that encourage us to be our best selves are hidden deep in the *Ted Lasso* DNA, there are motivational life lessons for women to be unearthed too. In their own separate styles, Rebecca and Keeley show us how to find resilience in the face of difficulty, how to be great leaders in the workplace, and how friendship can boost confidence and empower us.

Women thrive on strong female relationships. They are beneficial to our health, financial success, and even help us live longer. Encouraging each other builds self-confidence and makes challenges seem easier to overcome. Our superpower is each other.

"A lot of times TV starts women off in a competitive place, and then they figure out how to be friends. That's just not my experience in the workplace!" says Ashley Nicole Black, one of the show's writers and star of *A Black Lady Sketch Show.* "Especially working in Hollywood, where there aren't a lot of other women around. So, you find the only other one and say, 'Well, we have to be friends!' and you can get close pretty quickly, actually."

Hannah Waddingham and Juno Temple experienced that themselves when they began working on the show, becoming friends both on and off screen. "I get emotional talking about Juno, because she is without doubt the most sunshiny person…and she has come into my life and made me think to be a better person," says Hannah. "It's been fantastic to play two women that adore the bones of each other, who would trample anyone down to let the other one get ahead. I can only hope it will encourage a generation of young ladies to do the same."

Juno, in turn, describes Hannah in the same loving

way. "Female friendship is one of the most profoundly important things ever," she says. Like Hannah, Juno adored being part of a TV show that reflected that. "I think Rebecca is the first woman in Keeley's life to ever say: 'You actually have a really great brain. You should use it.' And Keeley reminds Rebecca it is okay to be vulnerable. They encourage each other to be the most exciting, fruitful, versions of themselves without being competitive."

From elementary school to college, girls outperform boys in academic work. They are more likely to get college degrees and less likely to drop out of education than men. But on average, women typically earn 80 percent of what men do if they are white, and 60 percent if they are of color ("2022 Women in the Workplace" study by McKinsey and Lean In). As of January 2023, women held only 28 percent of the board seats on publicly traded companies in the United States, made up only 28 percent of Congress and 25 percent of the Senate. Those percentages drop significantly for women of color. The UK, European, and Australian parliaments fare only marginally better.

The solution to those uncomfortable truth bombs is more women pulling each other up and helping each other along both in our personal and working lives. (The two are rarely separate if you are a woman.) Whether it is the gift that Keeley receives of a first edition of Jane Austen's *Sense and Sensibility*, a story of two sisters who learn from each other's best qualities, or Mae, the landlady at The Crown and Anchor pub, giving advice on being a boss, there are messages written into the show that support that idea.

TV shows have a long history of holding up a mirror. For every moment that Ted Lasso (played by Jason Sudeikis) redefines masculinity, admitting that he cries, loving romantic comedies, and confronting toxic masculinity, the show brings contemporary feminism into focus too. It gently nudges us to see what can happen when women support each other. Rebecca and Keeley are fabulous, relatable, uplifting female role models. They show us how by believing in each other, they become empowered.

Joining forces with psychologists, life coaches, female leaders, and the legend on whom Rebecca's character is loosely based, this unauthorized book is a fandom excursion into the *Ted Lasso* world, highlighting some of Rebecca's and Keeley's inspirational life lessons, showing how they relate to all of us, and the miraculous possibilities we have for change. It is a bucketload of wit, wisdom, and advice from some very smart women on how to find your inner lioness.

If you have not watched *Ted Lasso* on Apple TV+ yet, then stop reading here and turn on your TV or computer right now, first because you will not want to miss one of the best TV shows ever, but second because plot twists will be revealed.The use of the terms "women" and "female" is inclusive of anyone who identifies as that gender.

1
BE A GREAT GIRLFRIEND

"Never gonna give you up, never gonna let you down, never gonna turn around and desert you."

—Rick Astley

BEFORE WE EVEN meet Ted Lasso at the start of the first episode, we meet Rebecca, who is taking over her ex-husband's office at AFC Richmond, the soccer club he has lost to her in a divorce settlement. She is having his belongings boxed up when George Cartrick (played by Bill Fellows), the team coach, a man with a lecherous smirk and shorts that are too small for him, is ushered in."I love what you've done to the place," he says, his voice full of sarcasm. "Did you do it yourself or get some poof to help you?" Rebecca is not fazed, remarking that the same question could be asked of his hair.

"Right, love. I've got training in a minute, so whatever it is you need to get off your..." George gestures crudely at her breasts. "Impressive chest, let me have it." He is so cocksure of himself that he imagines he can patronize the woman who has just become his boss. He is so reckless with his derogatory, homophobic language that he cannot conceive that it might ever catch up with him.

But he has met his match in Rebecca. She fires him in one of the sharpest and funniest putdowns in TV history. Cool as the champagne in her fridge, she lists her reasons why, among them, his casual misogyny. "I know it's a big word," she says. "Ask one of your daughters what it means."

And so, the rallying cheer goes up from women everywhere. We are barely five minutes into the show, but we have already fallen in love with Rebecca. She is strong, quick-witted, and so powerful that Ted later remarks: "Boss, I tell you, I'd hate to see you and Michelle Obama arm wrestle." Rebecca is the kind of woman who seems to own a confidence we could all use.

It turns out, she is also a woman who might look tough, but like most of us, has her wounds. Rupert Mannion (played by Anthony Head), her ex, is a serial philanderer, whose cheating and lies have publicly humiliated her. He has used and discarded her, making tabloid headlines with his infidelity, leaving Rebecca lonely, hurt, and isolated. Her anger and hatred of him is what has got her through, and she is only enjoying ownership of the club because it was something that Rupert loved, and she intends to destroy it.

It takes Rebecca's friendship with Keeley for her

to start to heal. It is through a friendship with another woman that she gets a better perspective on her own life, restoring her self-esteem and finding love in her heart. Of course, Ted helps greatly in that too. This is the positive and optimistic world of *Ted Lasso,* after all, where "trickle-down economics might stink, but trickle-down support smells like pizza, roses, and Viola Davis." But when Rebecca veers too far off course in her mission of revenge, it is Keeley who ultimately holds her to account. It is "girl talk," and the kind of profound understanding that only someone of her own gender is able to offer, that makes a difference.

"I've decided to not be scared of you anymore," Keeley announces early in their friendship, throwing herself down next to Rebecca on the sofa in her office and kicking off her shoes. She gives Rebecca a cactus as a gift. "It's like you, strong and a bit prickly," she says.

Young, glamorous, and with a penchant for big earrings and topknot hairdos, Keeley is a girl who might have once had the pejorative label "WAG" (Wives and Girlfriends) attached to her name. It is a term the British tabloids frequently used for the female partners of professional soccer players during the 2000s. Victoria Beckham and Coleen Rooney were WAGs, always on the arms of their soccer player partners and being photographed by paparazzi. Keeley fits the mold, later describing herself as "famous for being almost famous."

She brings up how unkind the press were to Rebecca when Rupert cheated on her. "Didn't that make you really mad that they went after you and not Rupert?"

she asks. "*He* was the one that cheated but he came across as Prince Charming. It really pissed me off."

"The press are never awful to men," Rebecca agrees, referring to the double standards of the media where women are often made to look like sex objects. "No one pays a fortune for a picture of a naked man on his yacht in Majorca a week after his divorce."

The two women forge a solidarity, as many of us do, in comparing their experiences of living in an unequal world where discrimination filters into so much. Their friendship is further sealed when Keeley begs Rebecca to show her those pictures—the ones of Rebecca naked on a yacht taken by a paparazzo from a helicopter. Keeley is so complimentary of Rebecca's body that Rebecca cannot help but smile. Clearly, no one has given her a compliment for some time and Keeley's praise gives her a much-needed boost.

And that is the power of great female friends. They are the givers of compliments, the keepers of secrets, the boosters of confidence, the cheerleaders in our lives. They are the net to fall into when marriage or romance goes wrong. They are the truth tellers, the sex advisors, the relationship coaches, the nurturers, the listeners, the soothers, the entertainers, the drinking buddies, and the reliable source of tea, tissues, and cheer-up emojis. They are the source of sincere advice that you may not want to hear and the positive influencers when you need encouragement.

But there are other reasons why women need girlfriends. In 1992, a long-term study of the survival rates of breast cancer patients was set up, led by Candyce Kroenke, MPH, ScD, senior research scientist at the Kaiser Permanente Northern California Division of Research, checking in regularly with 2,835 women, all of whom had been diagnosed with stages 1 to 4 breast cancer. Ten years later, her study confirmed that the women who were socially isolated were more likely to die than those who had social ties. The study, the first of its kind, was indisputable proof that women need friends for their health ("Social Networks, Social Support, and Survival After Breast Cancer Diagnosis," *Journal of Clinical Oncology,* 2016). Other studies since have reached the same conclusion. Women with strong relationships are also less likely to suffer from depression and stress, according to *The American Journal of Psychiatry.*

The friendships do not necessarily have to be female. But when women look beyond their husbands and partners, they naturally gravitate toward friendships with other women. "Women are much more social in the way they cope with stress," explains psychologist Shelley E. Taylor, PhD, author of *The Tending Instinct: Women, Men, and the Biology of Relationships* (Holt). "Men are more likely to deal with stress with a 'fight or flight' reaction—with aggression or withdrawal. But aggression and withdrawal take a physiological toll, and friendship brings comfort that mitigates the ill effects of stress. That difference alone contributes to the gender difference in longevity."

All humans are hotwired to be social and connected with others. But for some reason, women seem to be better at it. Why? Clinical psychologist Bella Grossman at Northwell Health suggests it might be because women are raised differently. "Girls are encouraged more to share their feelings, to play interactively and cooperatively while boys are encouraged to play independently, competitively, and not to cry or share their feelings," she explains. "Given that female friendships typically discuss emotional experiences related to an event, friendships can help women to process their experience more deeply and obtain support to help reduce the negative impact of a chronic stressor."

In other words, when women talk about the difficult things they are going through, they internalize less, which seems to have a biological component. Scientists have been able to measure a reduction in cortisol, the harmful stress hormone, when women share their worries. They have also been able to see levels of oxytocin, the more beneficial hormone, being raised. "Research shows that women, possibly more than men, need to maintain connections, because they increase serotonin and oxytocin," says psychologist Alisa Ruby Bash, PsyD, LMFT. "And maintaining bonds becomes even more important as we grow older. We get busier, with more responsibilities. It makes us feel nurtured and validated to hang out with friends we can be totally ourselves with, minus the outside pressures."

Friendships grow from trust, each person coming to see the other as someone they can count on. At the benefit dinner that Rebecca hosts in the first season, Rebecca and Keeley meet again. This time they are on the red carpet, both looking their most glamorous. But Rebecca is nervous of posing in front of a horde of intimidating red carpet photographers. "I hate this bit," she says to Keeley, trying to maintain a camera-ready smile.

Keeley, who knows about modeling, comes to her aid, whispering some useful tricks and poses. Then she retreats behind the cameramen to yell, "Look at her, she's fit," which makes Rebecca laugh, and as a result, looks more relaxed and natural in the photos.

Now it is Rebecca's turn to do Keeley a favor, and Keeley's turn to reveal her own problems when they meet in the restroom later. A woman has outbid Keeley for her boyfriend, Jamie Tartt (played by Phil Dunster), at the auction where the prize is a night out with a soccer player. "I think you should know that the woman who was bidding on Jamie was his other plus-one," Rebecca reveals to her. Jamie had brought her along to make Keeley jealous. "Cheeky little prick," Keeley says.

We see, in that interaction, how Keeley could use a good friend too. She tells Rebecca that she started dating soccer players when she was eighteen but now that she is close to thirty, she is wondering why she is still doing it. We get the sense that Keeley is a little lost. Her career until now has been based mostly on her looks—a little bit of modeling, a little bit of branding or PR work—but mostly it has been centered around being photographed on the arm of celebrity soccer players. Now she is questioning how long she can keep doing that, especially if she must put up with an immature boyfriend who wants to make her jealous.

Rebecca brings up the subject of holding men accountable and shares her own painful story. "Everyone makes mistakes, but I was married to a man for twelve years who never once took responsibility for any single one of them," she says. By both women being open and honest, a trusting bond between them grows. Rebecca's courage lies not simply in leaving Rupert, but in sharing something deeply personal with Keeley. It proves to be a worthwhile risk, gaining her a friend. Sometimes it takes courage to embark on a new friendship.

"Rebecca and Keeley are pretty much polar opposites and don't realize that they need each other in order to flourish," Hannah Waddingham explains of the early episodes. "We find Rebecca at that position of brilliant businesswoman, very much at a loss socially, and the complete opposite for Keeley."

Besides the health benefits of friendship, there are many psychological benefits too. Researchers at the University of Virginia set up an experiment to see if friendship alters how we approach challenges in our daily lives. They asked thirty-four students to stand at the base of a steep hill wearing a backpack filled with weights. Some of the students were alone, while others were in pairs. Each of the students imagined they were going to be asked to climb the hill, but in fact, the researchers just wanted them to estimate how steep the climb would be.

The astonishing result was that the students who were on their own perceived the hill to be steeper and much harder to climb, but those who were with a friend gave lower estimates of the gradient and imagined it easier to climb. It also turned out, the longer the two friends had known each other, the less steep the hill appeared to be to them ("Social Support and the Perception of Geographical Slant," *National Library of Medicine*).

That's mind-boggling proof of the power of friendship. As a result of Rebecca's insight and support in the restroom, Keeley finds the strength to walk away from her immature boyfriend, precisely modeling that "Perception of Geographical Slant" study. With a friend's backing, the challenge of breaking up with Jamie felt less frightening to her. The hill she needed to climb seemed less steep. Would she have found the courage to walk away from him without Rebecca?

Over the three seasons, there are many other examples where Rebecca and Keeley's support of each other makes them braver. There is only one moment of duplicity between the two women. And it is an important one because it demonstrates how good friends also hold each other to account, which in turn can make the friendship stronger still.

Rebecca had commissioned a paparazzo to follow Ted, hoping to get a compromising photo of him that could be used to publicly humiliate him in the papers. (This was a weapon that she had been the victim of herself during her divorce from Rupert.) She was on her ill-conceived revenge mission to destroy AFC Richmond at the time, and did not care how many people got hurt in the process of damaging her ex. Given how honest Ted is, the plan was never likely to succeed, but on the set of a vodka commercial where Keeley is doing some modeling, the paparazzo gets an opportunity to snap a photo of Ted and Keeley together which could be misconstrued as compromising.

When Keeley discovers that it was Rebecca who had commissioned the paparazzo as part of her revenge plans, she confronts Rebecca head-on. She demands Rebecca apologize to Ted. By now Keeley and Rebecca's friendship is well established. There is a familiarity between them that is as warm and comfortable as a pair of slippers. But all of that is threatened suddenly.

"Imagine doing something unforgivable, to someone who doesn't deserve it, then having to look them in the eye and telling them what you've done," Rebecca says desperately to Keeley. "Why tell him?"

Keeley's response is swift and apt. "It would change how *I* feel about you," she responds. And there it is. In that split second, Rebecca understands that it is her standing in Keeley's eyes that is at stake. She might get away with not confessing or apologizing to Ted, but she will not get away with it with Keeley. It is out of respect for Keeley and seeing the value of their friendship that Rebecca comes to be not only more honest with Ted, but more importantly, with herself. Female friendships do that. It is why they are important.

HOW TO MAKE FEMALE FRIENDS (AS A GROWN WOMAN)

Sometimes we relocate and find ourselves looking for new friends. But it is not always easy. Here's a few ideas:

1. Join volunteer groups. It is the superfood of positive psychology, and you will bond with others instantly.
2. Be curious, not judgmental. If you talk to people, friendships grow.
3. Sign up for friend matchmaking sites like *www.girlfriendsocial.com.*
4. Take evening classes at your local community college.
5. Be courageous like the lioness you are and reach out.
6. When you see another woman succeed, do not be jealous. Befriend her.

ADVICE FROM THE SISTERHOOD

"Abandon the cultural myth that all female friendships must be bitchy, toxic, or competitive. This myth is designed to SLOW women down."

—ROXANE GAY, WRITER, PROFESSOR, AND AUTHOR OF THE NEW YORK TIMES BEST-SELLING BAD FEMINIST

"Friendships between women, as any woman will tell you, are built of a thousand small kindnesses… swapped back and forth and over again."

—MICHELLE OBAMA, ATTORNEY, AUTHOR, AND FORMER FIRST LADY OF THE UNITED STATES FROM 2009 TO 2017

"Women's friendships are like a renewable source of power."

—JANE FONDA, ACTRESS, ACTIVIST "

Surround yourself with somebody who is as happy for your happiness as you are for your happiness."

—OPRAH WINFREY, TALK SHOW HOST, PRODUCER, ACTRESS, AUTHOR, AND MEDIA PROPRIETOR, REFLECTING ON HER FORTY-FIVE YEAR FRIENDSHIP WITH AUTHOR AND JOURNALIST GAYLE KING

"I don't know what I would have done if I hadn't had my girlfriends. They have literally gotten me up out of bed, put me in the shower, dressed me, said, 'Hey, you can do this,' and pushed me out the door!"

—Reese Witherspoon, actress and producer

"Well, my very favorite person, and I love her as a person as well as a singer, I think she's the greatest, and that's Ella Fitzgerald."

—Marilyn Monroe on her friendship with Ella Fitzgerald, who had been struggling to get gigs because of racism when they met. Monroe famously promised the owner of the Mocambo, a Los Angeles club, that she'd sit in the front row and bring her famous friends, like Frank Sinatra and Judy Garland, if he booked Fitzgerald. The show instantly sold out

"Marilyn has a heart of gold. She was a true friend who believed in me and helped break down barriers in an industry that wasn't always fair."

—Ella Fitzgerald, singer, "First Lady of Song," "Queen of Jazz"

"Women understand. We may share experiences, make jokes, paint pictures, and describe humiliations that mean nothing to men, but women understand. The odd thing about these deep and personal connections of women is that they often ignore barriers of age, economics, worldly experience, race, culture—all the barriers that, in male or mixed society, had seemed so difficult to cross."

—Gloria Steinem, journalist,
social-political activist

"Some women pray for their daughters to marry good husbands. I pray that my girls will find girlfriends half as loyal and true as the Ya-Yas."

—Rebecca Wells, actor, playwright, and
author of the *Ya-Ya Sisterhood* series

2

BE A MENTOR

"A good mentor hopes you will move on.
A great mentor knows you will."

—Leslie Higgins

"MEN GIVE EACH other jobs in the toilets all the time," Rebecca tells Keeley. There is humor to the line, of course, but also another of what Ted would call a truth bomb.

Keeley has been working on some PR branding for her now-former boyfriend, Jamie Tartt. Rebecca asks if she would be interested in a job at AFC Richmond doing the same for some of the other players. Keeley is hesitant, insisting that Rebecca does not need to do that just because she was kind to her in the restroom the other night. But Rebecca tells her that is what men do all the time. And she is right.

Men gravitate to sponsoring and mentoring other

men who they connect with more naturally all the time. They are not only more likely to give each other jobs, they are also more likely to give each other promotions, pay raises, and some hearty slaps on the back. It is one of the hardest barriers that women face in the employment market. And because there are not enough women in senior positions to do the same for the girls, the situation calls for Dr. Sharon's seminal line: "The truth will set you free, but first it will piss you off."

Only one in four top management executives (sometimes called "C-suite" executives; the "C" stands for chief) are women, and only one in twenty is a woman of color, according to the 2022 Women in the Workplace study, the largest comprehensive initiative looking at women in corporate America, published annually by McKinsey and Lean In. In the study the researchers also found that for every 100 men who are promoted from entry level to manager, only eighty-seven women and only eighty-two women of color also make it. The further up the leadership chain you go, the less women you will see.

What makes those statistics worthy of more expletives than even Roy Kent (played by Brett Goldstein) could muster, is that the women who are being overlooked are likely to be equally or better qualified than their male counterparts ("2022 Women in Workplace" study). They are more likely to have performed better and achieved higher grades in school and college (Pew Research Center) and demonstrate more transformational leadership styles, according to the American Psychological Association ("Gender and the Evaluation of Leaders: A

Meta-analysis"). But because women remain in the minority in senior workplace positions, there is not the network of other well-connected female peers to help them along.

"Men have an easier time finding the mentors and sponsors who are invaluable for career progression," explains Sheryl Sandberg, formerly chief operating officer of Meta and author of the bestseller *Lean In: Women, Work, and the Will to Lead* (Alfred A. Knopf). "Women face real obstacles in the professional world, including blatant and subtle sexism, discrimination, and sexual harassment. Too few places offer flexibility and access to childcare... Plus women have to prove themselves to a far greater extent than men."

Sandberg wrote her acclaimed book more than a decade ago. It sold over four million copies in less than five years and brought much-needed attention to the harsh reality that women were being overlooked in the workplace. In subsequent years, the book has had its critics, some of whom question Sandberg's approach, which places the responsibility of changing the status quo on individual women rather than on society and workplaces, which of course also needs addressing.

But there is no disputing that Sandberg shone a light on an issue that still remains. "Despite modest gains in representation over the last eight years, women—especially women of color—are still drastically underrepresented in corporate America," states the 2022 Women in the Workplace study.

So, when Rebecca offers Keeley a job, a woman sponsoring another woman in the workplace, it is a big hurray moment because it helps to normalize and promote the idea of women supporting women. It highlights a solution to a really difficult problem for women. It also creates a vision for the way it could be in the real world. "Women can accomplish amazing things when we support each other," Sandberg says. Her foundation now supports more than 35,000 female networking groups called Lean In Circles in 160 countries. "The more women help one another, the more we help ourselves. Acting like a coalition truly does produce results," she says.

When Keeley then pays it forward to her old friend Shandy (played by Ambreen Razia) with a job in the third season, that is precisely how it is meant to work too. Building confidence and success in junior women has a ripple effect—one woman's advancement helps everyone else. (Unfortunately, paying it forward with Shandy does not work out well when she turns out to be an unreliable employee. This is a comedy, after all.)

Rebecca inspires Keeley, advising her, and showing her what it takes to be a female leader in business, while Keeley helps Rebecca by bringing her marketing and PR skills to make her business grow. AFC Richmond gains especially when Keeley brings the sponsorship of the dating app Bantr to the club, and Rebecca gains by having a trusted opinion in her decision-making process. Both women win. And that is the beauty of mentorships and sponsorships.

A workforce analytics study into the advantages of mentorship was set up at the American tech firm Sun

Microsystems in 2006. More than 1,000 employees were followed over a five-year period comparing the career advancement of those who took part in the company's mentoring program and those who did not. They found that those who took part had a salary increase and were promoted five times more often than those who did not.

"The truth is it actually feels good to help other women and you also learn from the people you mentor," explains Robyn Foyster, editor of *Women Love Tech, The Carousel* and *Game Changers,* and founder of thought leadership agency InProfile who has mentored many women.

"Often, the support from a mentor can be the very thing that gives someone the motivation and inspiration to succeed. In my earlier career, the word mentoring was not really a thing. There was no formal training but rather a sink or swim career ride that was bumpy at times. So, it's really good to see that this has changed, typified by a woman like Keeley getting a makeover that helps propel her ahead in business not just getting the Cinderella make-over cliché. Rebecca really nurtures Keeley's career. I hope it gives encouragement to other women to do the same."

Strictly speaking, Rebecca sponsors Keeley when she gives her a job and then mentors her when she offers career advice. There are subtle differences in the definitions, but the important point is mentorships and sponsorships can boost a career. There are just not enough of them available to women.

"You helped this panda become a lion," Keeley tells Rebecca at the end of the second season. She has learned so much working for Rebecca that she has been featured as "Keeley Jones, Woman on Top" in a fictional issue of *Vanity Fair* magazine and offered the chance to launch her own business. It is a sweet moment with both women in tears because now Keeley must move on. Rebecca is thrilled for her, of course. And Keeley is grateful to Rebecca for the opportunity she gave her. But it is a makeover that is as ingenious as the show.

In so many films and TV shows, women and girls get the outdated Cinderella makeover cliché, their transformations resolved with a new outfit or hair. That stereotype does not do women favors. Much as we might love a new lipstick, pair of heels, or a fabulous new dress (nothing wrong with that at all), we are so much more than that.

The best makeover stories for women are the ones where we get ahead, not because of how we look, but for what we are capable of and our achievements. Keeley's makeover from panda to lioness is the story of a woman discovering that she is much more than her looks. Her intelligence, marketing skills, business savvy, compassion, and positivity are what make her majestic.

HOW TO FIND A MENTOR IN BUSINESS

1. Ask good questions. Sometimes you can stand out from others by simply asking thoughtful questions.
2. Demonstrate your usefulness and problem-solving powers. A potential mentor will be interested in how you can help them.
3. Be positive like Ted or Keeley. Everyone has their stresses at work. You will gain more attention in the workplace for being the smiling face in the room.
4. Increasing numbers of companies are starting mentorship programs after seeing their advantages. Search diligently to find them.
5. Join women's networking groups like Lean In Circles, Senior Equity Lounges (The Female Quotient), and Allbright Alliance events. (See reference pages for details.)
6. Be coachable and prepared to listen. Remember to pay it forward. Help those who are junior to you.

3
BE AMBITIOUS

"Being a boss has its moments. But for some it's better to follow your gut."

—Mae, landlady at The Crown and Anchor for forty years

REBECCA IS WEARING an eggplant-colored suit and a practiced fearless smile. She is being photographed for a magazine, posing against the backdrop of the AFC Richmond locker room. "Watch your back, Kate Moss, there's a new bad girl on the British modeling scene," jokes Ted as he bounds in, offering encouragement and his famous biscuits. "You get nervous doing this kind of stuff?" he asks her more seriously when the shoot is over.

The photo is for a "Women in Football" profile in a fictional financial magazine, but Rebecca dismisses it as not a big deal. Ted disagrees. "Oh, come on, now. Being a role model is a huge deal. Don't you realize that there's probably a little girl out there somewhere rocking a tiny eggplant-colored power suit, and she's just dreaming about becoming a sports executive someday. She's gonna read this article and she's gonna think, 'Holy smokes, my dreams are possible.' "

Ted is 100 percent right on that. Girls need role models. We cannot be what we cannot see. Rebecca is a woman at the height of her power leading not just a soccer club, not just a business, but a team that is composed entirely of men. Of course we need her as a role model.

But in real life, Rebecca is a rarity. Female sports executives or women on the boards of sports teams are few and far between. Only 11 percent of board members at British Premier League soccer clubs are women, according to Fairgame in their 2022 report "The Gender Divide That Fails Football's Bottom Line: The Commercial Case for Gender Equality." Women CEOs of sports teams are even scarcer—that is true whether you search in the UK, US, Australia, Europe, or anywhere else. But there are a few of them, including one powerful woman on whom Rebecca's character is loosely based.

Rebecca tantalizingly slips the first names of three other women into that scene as Easter eggs for us to find. She tells Ted that "Delia, Karren, and Posh Spice" are also being profiled as "Women in Football." Although the magazine is fictional, the women she mentions are not. Each is a real-life role model with an inspiring story of her own.

"Delia" refers to Delia Smith, known as the "Queen

of Cookery" in Britain, a woman who became one of the country's first celebrity TV chefs during the Seventies, hailed and adored for her common-sense approach to food. She is also an author, and most relevant, a joint majority shareholder of the soccer club Norwich City FC.

Delia left school without any qualifications at the age of sixteen, took a job washing dishes in a restaurant, learned to cook, and began writing articles about food in newspapers. Ambitious and keen to forge her own path, she parlayed her cookery writing into presenting recipes on TV, eventually becoming so famous that when she recommended a certain ingredient in her dishes, the supermarkets would often sell out.

Watching soccer was always a love for her, and when her favorite soccer team, Norwich City FC, was on the brink of bankruptcy in 1996, she saw an investment opportunity, negotiating two seats on the board, one for herself and one for her husband. She is now in her eighties and can still be seen at every match. The club has been promoted to the Premier League five times since she took charge (also relegated at times), but in every respect, she is a woman who has built a career on her own terms in a world where women are rarely welcomed.

"Posh Spice" is Victoria Beckham, arguably the original WAG. She was once famous for being a member of the girl pop group Spice Girls and for dating former top soccer player David Beckham, to whom she is now married, with four children. But it is her later career that is so impressive, living out the lyrics of the group's debut empowerment song "Wannabe."

After the Spice Girls split, she began designing her own clothes and eventually launched her own luxury ready-to-wear fashion label in 2008, and a subsequent, more affordable line in 2011. Her global fashion and beauty empire is now worth millions. Through her talent and ambition, she went from WAG to highly respected business tycoon.

"Karren" refers to the remarkable Baroness Karren Brady, informally known as "The First Lady of Football," who is probably the closest to a real-life Rebecca that we are ever likely to find. She is currently vice chairman of West Ham United FC, responsible for turning around the fortunes of the club when it was facing enormous debts. She was also the first woman to ever hold a senior management position in a Premier League soccer club, and has become a television personality, a mother, a champion of women in business, a motivational speaker, a member of Britain's House of Lords and author of several books, including the bestseller *Strong Woman: Ambition, Grit, and a Great Pair of Heels* (HarperCollins).

No surprise that Hannah Waddingham studied Baroness Brady when she was researching how she might play Rebecca. "I was very aware that she has never once apologized for her femininity or her sexuality," Hannah explains. "I watched a lot of videos of her, of how she carries herself, even her hand gestures, the angle of her head, just in terms of making people stand up and listen."

Just as Rebecca does in *Ted Lasso*, Baroness Brady holds herself always with the stature of authority. She is a woman who commands a room. At the age of twenty-three, Karren Brady persuaded her boss, who ran a newspaper, to invest in a rundown soccer club that was on the verge of bankruptcy, which she had seen for sale in the *Financial Times*. She was a young woman who was driven by a strong desire to be financially independent. She saw money as power, and she liked to work hard. So, she told her boss that if he bought the club and made her CEO, she would make the club profitable for him. Birmingham City FC was bought for $870,000 (£700,000) in 1993 and sold for $116 million (£93 million) sixteen years later. By the time Baroness Brady left the club, 75 percent of senior management were women, and she was established as a respected CEO.

Baroness Brady did not know much about soccer, but she knew about ambition, one of her favorite subjects to talk about. "If someone talks about an ambitious man, you conjure up the image of a dynamic go-getter... someone in control; a man going places, someone to admire," she says. "Yet exactly the opposite happens if you mention an ambitious woman. If they're honest, a lot of people immediately think, 'I bet she's a right hard-nosed bitch!' We have to change that thinking. In the same way, we have to change the perception of feminism... A feminist is not someone who burns her bra and hates men. A feminist is simply someone who actively promotes the belief that women are equal to men."

A female CEO of a soccer club was such a rarity when Baroness Brady started out that she was regularly directed to the "Wives of the Directors" box at soccer grounds because no one would believe she was a director herself. She even had opposition fans chanting "Karren Brady is a whore," and a player, whom she employed, dare to say to her face, "I can see your tits in that top." (She later passed him onto another club, because being the boss, she had that power.)

But she refused to be intimidated and continues to lead in business. Now in her fifties, she has worked to change the way people perceive working women, arguing the need for more women in boardrooms, for greater flexibility for women in the workplace, equal pay, greater support for childcare, more help from governments, and of course, a change in attitudes so that women are free to enter professions that have traditionally been framed as male.

"I am independent, driven, and motivated. I have taught myself to rely on no one but myself. I don't pretend to be someone I'm not. I have self-esteem, and I know that I'm capable of achieving anything I put my mind to," she says. "If you don't champion your career, who will do it for you?"

Baroness Brady has never apologized for being who she is. From her killer arched eyebrows to her steely disposition, she remains a woman who commands respect for who she is and her extraordinary level of achievement. Of course Hannah Waddingham studied her.

HOW TO GROW THE MINDSET OF BARONESS KARREN BRADY:

1. Have confidence. "I have never let people put me down."
2. Stand up for yourself. "I have never been particularly worried about offending people."
3. Speak plainly. "There's no need to be rude but sometimes plain speaking is the only answer."
4. Build self-esteem. "Self-esteem eliminates fear."
5. Personality is important. "A bit of presence or charm."
6. Promote from within. "I like to mentor and guide my staff to be the best they can be."
7. Love problems and challenges. "Life is a series of problems. How happy you are relates to the solutions you find to deal with them."
8. Work hard. "If you want to be successful, you have to graft." (British phrase meaning work hard)
9. Be ambitious. "I'm ambitious, but I've never seen that as requiring me to be nasty."
10. Be loyal. "Loyalty is created by mutual respect, by promoting people and allowing them to take credit for their work."
11. Quotes from *Strong Woman: Ambition, Grit and a Great Pair of Heels* By Karren Brady *(HarperCollins):*

4

BE POSITIVE AND EMPATHETIC

"Bit of advice for being a boss. Hire your best friend."

—Rebecca to Keeley

AND WHAT ABOUT Keeley? Keeley is open, loud, and loving. She is unpretentious, energetic, and a fabulous, fun dresser. We love her fake fur coats, her vertiginous platforms, her animal print dresses, all forty-four of her different hairstyles (yes, there were that many), her worship of pink, especially that pen with a fluffy bit on the end, and her ceramic leopard, Frenchie.

She is a woman with a defiant style of her own and every inch an independent woman, which she makes clear to Roy before they go on a date. Her story arc is a girl once recognized for her looks and association with soccer players who becomes her own boss. That is worthy of applause.

There has been much speculation about who Keeley might be modeled on in real life. Victoria Beckham has been suggested; Keeley Hazell, a former topless model who became an actress and stars in *Ted Lasso* as Bex, Rupert's new wife, is another possibility. But neither quite fit. Perhaps we will never know. Juno Temple has said she never wants to share who inspires her when she plays Keeley: "There is a woman in my life who is one of my best, best, best friends, who has been a big part of my inspiration for Keeley, because she is somebody who, in the most extraordinary way, always manages to bring a little bit of light everywhere she goes, but I like to keep who she is secret."

If Ted is the male poster child for alacrity and encouragement of those around him, Keeley is the female version. She mirrors Ted's positivity and goodwill. She is always curious about others, has a terrific understanding of people, and brings out the best in others. She is also ambitious. When she takes Nate Shelley (played by Nick Mohammed) shopping for a new suit in the second season, she confides in him: "I used to worry I'd end up becoming my mom," adding that her mom spent years working at the same company without complaint while a man took all the credit. It is a story that many women will be familiar with, but Keeley is not prepared to do the same. "She wasn't brave enough to dream big, so I decided to do things differently," Keeley says. "Then I met Rebecca, and she inspired me to want to be a boss."

It is such a hopeful dream, and she is such a sweet-natured, sunny character that by the third season when she becomes her own boss, we are rooting for her. "You deserve this," Rebecca tells her, and we would say the same.

We might also remark on the way she runs her company. Remember how she took Barbara (played by Katy Wix), the chief financial officer at KJPR, her public relations firm, aside after she had humiliated her old friend Shandy? Keeley had just hired Shandy to work there, but Barbara did not approve and made it plain. "Barbara, the way you just treated Shandy was incredibly rude," Keeley tells her. "It was hurtful… You cannot speak to people like that… I believe in her." Keeley gets a little side-tracked with Barbara's snow globe collection at this point, but then she delivers. "Maybe you and I can see how it feels to believe in someone else together."

Believing in others and leading with empathy builds teams and productivity. When people treat each other with respect and approach interactions with the intent to learn and understand, organizations see not only increases in productivity and performance, but also improvements in team morale, communication, and growth, according to the 2022 Women Business Leaders Outlook Study (KPMG). Employees who see their leaders demonstrate empathy, defined as the ability to understand another's feelings, are then more likely to express it themselves.

Empathetic leadership has become the holy grail in business if companies want to retain motivated and happy team members. And women, it turns out, are really, really, really (keep saying "really") good at it.

"Scientific studies have consistently shown that on

the most key traits that make leaders more effective, women tend to outperform men. For example, humility, self-awareness, self-control, moral sensitivity, social skills, emotional intelligence, kindness, a prosocial and moral orientation are more likely to be found in women than men," says organizational psychologist Dr. Tomas Chamorro-Premuzic, professor of business psychology at University College London and author of *Why Do So Many Incompetent Men Become Leaders?* (Harvard Business Review Press).

"Women also outperform men in educational settings, while men score higher than women on dark side personality traits, such as aggression, narcissism, psychopathy, and Machiavellianism, which account for much of the toxic and destructive behaviors displayed by powerful men."

The best proof of the power of empathetic female leadership in the real world happened during the first Covid-19 pandemic year when crisis management and good leadership was imperative for survival in 194 countries around the world. Of 194 independent countries, nineteen had female leaders at the time—women like President Jacinda Ardern in New Zealand, Chancellor Angela Merkel in Germany, and Prime Minister Mette Frederiksen in Denmark. All the women leaders had different economies and recourses available to them, but they were each faced with the same threat as the male leaders of countries—a killer virus. How each of those 175 men and nineteen women reacted tells a significant story.

Every country that was led by a woman had significantly better Covid-19 outcomes. Specifically, their countries reported many fewer deaths than those countries led by men. That is not a fairy tale, nor politics, nor a sitcom storyline. It is a statistical study carried out by the World Economic Forum ("An Analysis of 194 Countries," published by the Centre for Economic Policy Research and the World Economic Forum). It is a great example of how women assess risk, react quickly, and solve problems with compassion, empathy, and a long-term view in mind.

"Women are more likely to lead democratically, show transformational leadership, be a role model, listen to others and develop their subordinates' potential and score higher on measures of leadership potential," says Tomas Chamorro-Premuzic. "So an obvious question arises: if women have more potential for leadership, then why are they still the minority group among leaders?"

Perhaps the writers of the show were asking themselves the same excellent question. It is estimated that the world's GDP (Gross Domestic Product) is $12 trillion lower today than it might be if there were greater gender equality and more women leaders (McKinsey). Perhaps the writers of the show wanted to present an alternative possibility.

HOW TO BE A GREAT LEADER: THE KEELEY WAY

1. Be positive and spread sunshine.
2. Remember to praise the poets and geniuses on your team.
3. Give people a chance and believe in others.
4. Learn to give the compliment sandwich—two compliments wrapped around a critical truth.
5. Admit openly when you do not know something.
6. Trust your intuition in your decision making.
7. Avoid romance in the workplace (that was such a mistake, Keeley!)
8. Buy a unicorn notebook and record your triumphs.
9. Be prepared to muck in—even if it means cleaning up sheep poo.
10. Be kind.

5

BE VULNERABLE AND THINK FOR THE LONG TERM

"You're amazing. Let's invade France."

—Keeley to Rebecca

REBECCA HAS A business decision to make. Sam Obisanya (played by Toheeb Jimoh) has taken a stand against AFC Richmond's corporate sponsor, the fictional Dubai Air. The airline is owned by Cerithium Oil, also a fictional company, that is causing economic devastation in Nigeria where Sam is from, so he has pulled out of his sponsorship deal with them. It is a move that gets support from the rest of the team, but now Rebecca must deal with the fallout. What is she going to do now that Dubai Air is demanding that she fire Sam? The airline is threatening to withdraw much-needed sponsorship money from the club if she does not do as it asks.

Besides being a perfect moment of TV tension, it also calls for leadership and Rebecca delivers a textbook example of how a woman very often leads with vulnerability, admitting she might not have all the answers herself, seeking the advice of others and taking a longer-term view that goes beyond short-term profits. "Women are more likely to include varied perspectives in decision making and as a result are better at empathizing with both colleagues and customers. They often lead with vulnerability and a willingness to ignore expectations and to do things their own way," explains Julia Boorstin, CNBC's senior media & tech correspondent, and author of *When Women Lead: What They Achieve, Why They Succeed, How We Can Learn from Them* (Avid Reader Press).

Rebecca does precisely this. On the day that she must decide whether to fire Sam to keep her sponsorship money or lose him, she has her teenage goddaughter Nora (played by Kiki May) shadowing her in her workday. She shares the situation and it is Nora's influence that helps her. "Sometimes you have to do the right thing, even if you lose," Nora says. Rebecca listens, telling the CEO of Cerithium Oil that she will not be firing Sam, signing her email memorably as "Boss Ass Bitch."

It is of course some stretch to imagine that it is the advice of a teenager that seals her decision. But it demonstrates how Rebecca seeks the advice of others (usually Ted, Higgins, and Keeley) when she has tough decisions to make. She is not a leader who allows her ego to get in her way.

Her decision is also the right one because Rebecca knows that Sam is a valuable player for the team. She might lose some sponsorship money if she keeps him, but in the long term, if she does not keep him, she would lose more. Sponsorship money is replaceable, but superstar soccer players (whom you might also have a soft spot in your heart for) are harder to replace. Sam's playing will add value to the club in the long term.

Staying loyal and protective of your team is also essential, and by the third season, Bantr is sponsoring the team instead of Dubai Air and AFC Richmond is worth so much that we get to see Rebecca spit out her drink from shock when she discovers its potential price tag. Her decision had paid off.

Julia Boorstin interviewed more than 120 women leaders for her book, including many who ran Fortune 500 companies. She found that these women had built strong companies with smart teams behind them. Like Rebecca, these women were great communicators and nurtured loyalty. They listened to employees and studied research. They were versatile, cool-headed in risk taking, hard-working, and innovative.

"Over the course of countless interviews, I was struck by a unique approach to leadership which many of these women were taking," says Boorstin. "I saw them solving problems and creating products they wanted or needed that didn't yet exist. They were finding opportunities that men had overlooked. From Bumble, which inverted the power dynamics of online dating, to the biotech company LanzaTech, which turns pollution into fuel, women were creating and leading some of the most disruptive and innovative businesses."

They were also frequently leading with vulnerability, a trait that has become a buzzword among leadership training programs, highly regarded, not as a weakness, but as a power. Vulnerability is about being open, honest, and exposing ourselves, even our weaknesses, and by doing this we create trust. By sharing who we really are and admitting if we are uncertain about something, it allows us to connect with others and builds stronger, more trusting relationships. It works in business and in our personal lives too, which psychologist Brené Brown, research professor at the University of Houston, talks about in her famous TED talk and audiobook *The Power of Vulnerability.*

"Vulnerability invites trust and collaboration," explains Boorstin. "Its opposite—an attitude of invincibility—has been found to prevent leaders from receiving vital feedback and leads to what academics call 'opinion conformity.' A study found that high levels of flattery increase CEOs' overconfidence in their judgment and leadership capability. No surprise, overconfidence is found to result in biased decision making—and that drives under performance."

As the seasons progress, Rebecca discovers that she is actually good at her job. She might have thought she was simply taking over from her ex-husband, Rupert, as the club owner in the first season, but she increasingly hits her stride. She had been brave enough, *vulnerable enough,* to share her fears and worries with Ted, and in so doing, won his loyalty and support. But by the third season, her mettle gets tested again, and now we see how powerful and effective she has become.

When Rupert invites her to a lunch with an exclusive band of soccer club CEOs, including the billionaire Edwin Akufo (played by Sam Richardson), who wants to create the Akufo League, a super league of soccer's top clubs, Rebecca understands that it is an elitist move he is proposing. It will lead to more money for the club owners but make the tickets more expensive for fans.

She is uncertain at first about going to the lunch and asks Higgins (played by Jeremy Swift) for his opinion. "Is it because Akufo is an emotionally erratic billionaire with the temperament of one of those kids in *Willy Wonka*?" he asks. No, that's not her reasoning, though we can all see Higgins's point. She is concerned that she is only being invited because it will make the league look politically correct to have a woman there. (Reality check, anyone?) Higgins persuades her to at least listen to what is being proposed.

"How could I resist having a bunch of old men speak directly to my chest?" she concedes.

We are glad she goes because it becomes Rebecca's finest hour, the moment when she becomes a warrior princess single-handedly defending a castle in the face of marauders. Like Queen Boudicca going into battle to save what she believes in, she is lion-hearted and fearless, and refuses to toe the line in what is presented as a greedy male-dominated world."How much more money do you need?" she demands of the fat-cat billionaires sitting around her, comfortable in their exaggerated sense of male superiority, their indifference to any other path beyond avarice.

Rebecca knows the heartbreak and cost a super league will create for her club's fans. She is aware of the potential damage to the game itself and her business in the long term. But her strength is more than just in her bravery for being there, it is in persuading the men in the room to change their minds. Power around a conference table, as women know, is not about who can shout the loudest or flex the most muscles; it is an ability to present a convincing argument. It is about changing mindsets, thinking intelligently, and winning.

In a potent speech, Rebecca reminds us of a woman's power. She convinces the men that soccer was a game they once loved, and the short-term profit of a super league would harm the game in the long term, destroying everything. Would a male leader think that far ahead?

HOW TO BE A GREAT LEADER: THE REBECCA WAY

1. Avoid channeling male behaviors intentionally or unintentionally. You are you. Trust that.
2. Own up to your mistakes and make apologies where necessary. (Especially to Ted and Higgins.)
3. Allow others to be smarter than you. You will learn from them.
4. Get to know your team's strengths and weaknesses. It is useful knowledge.
5. Share your own vulnerabilities. It builds trust.
6. Build a network of strong women around you.
7. Do not be afraid to speak your mind. (Even if it means going into the gents' toilets to do it.)
8. Take a long-term view over short-term profit.
9. Never compromise your femininity.
10. Be brave in the boardroom. (Even if you are the only woman there.)

6
BE RESILIENT

"Shit helps things grow."

—Mae,
landlady at The Crown and Anchor

POOR KEELEY! SHE has lost her boyfriend, Roy, *and* her business. She is sitting at the bar of The Crown and Anchor, asking Mae (played by Annette Badland), the landlady, what is the opposite of the Midas touch? The Midas shits, Mae tells her, when everything you touch turns to shit.

Sometimes it is easy to feel that way because the odds are still stacked against women. Lower rates of career advancement, lower pay, lack of venture capital funding, and the responsibility of childcare remaining firmly on female shoulders conspire against women, according to the 2022 Women in the Workplace stud*y* (McKinsey and Lean In). Since the pandemic of 2020, women are also reporting alarmingly high levels of burnout.

When we see Keeley struggling, it is an opportunity to reflect on female resilience, and remind ourselves that sometimes we need to be steadfast in our ambitions, no matter what. First, let's consider Roy.

At the end of the second season, he presents Keeley with a gift on her last day at AFC Richmond—two tickets to Marbella for a six-week vacation in a villa by the sea. Keeley has just been given the opportunity of a lifetime with venture capital funding to open her own public relations firm, KJPR. Her dream to be her own boss is about to come true.

But for some ill-thought, tone-deaf reason, Roy thinks it is time for a vacation. "Are you out of your mind, Roy?" we want to yell at him. We see the shadows of conflict cloud Keeley's face as she works out how to tell him that as romantic as the gesture is, she cannot possibly go. "I'd love to go, but I can't," she says. "I don't start work in six weeks. I started a week ago."

Unafraid of hard work, Keeley recognizes what needs to be done if she is to prove herself. This is what it takes to be your own boss. What makes the storyline authentic is that it hits on a touchy subject—can a male partner recognize that a woman's career is as important for her as his is to him?

Roy seems to think that if Keeley does not want to go to Marbella with him, it must be because she does not want to be with him. "Are we breaking up?" he asks her. Of course, that is not why she cannot go. She simply needs to put her career first right now. It does not mean she does not love him. She is just doing what she needs to do for herself.

But Roy cannot cope with this. The next time we see Keeley, we learn that she and Roy *have* broken up. "We're too busy," Roy explains to his niece Phoebe (played by Elodie Blomfield) in the third season. "Keeley's got her own company now and that takes up a lot of her time and focus." Later, we learn that it was Roy who broke up with Keeley and although it is never fully explained, all the clues suggest that Roy did not want Keeley to devote so much time and effort to her business. Perhaps he wanted her to devote more time to him.

Can you have an egalitarian partnership with a husband or boyfriend where both careers are taken equally seriously? For many women, the answer is no. A study of 25,000 male and female Harvard Business School graduates over two decades, found that 40 percent of Generation X and Baby Boomer women believed their spouses' careers took priority over their own ("Rethink What You Know About High Achieving Women," *Harvard Business Review*). Meanwhile, 70 percent of Generation X and Boomer men said their careers were more important than those of their wives.

The sad takeaway of that 2014 study was that, when further questioned, the majority of the women had not expected it to turn out that way when they embarked on their relationships. They imagined their own careers would be equally important. But lack of career progression, making childcare arrangements, earning less than their male partners, contributed to their dreams and ambitions being put on the back shelf to make way for their spouse's.

Nearly a decade later, Deloitte's 2023 Women at Work study reported little change. Their survey of 5,000 women across ten countries found that women still bear most of the responsibility for domestic work and child-care. More than a third of the women they surveyed felt the need to prioritize their partner's career over their own. Their biggest reason was because their male partners earned more money. You will remember the important statistic that is worth repeating loud and often: women in America still earn, on average, only eighty cents for every dollar a man makes, sixty cents if you are a woman of color. (There are variances of the gender pay gap in different countries.)

But let's get back to Keeley. Even though prioritizing her career has been at the cost of her relationship, she carries on. Of course she does. Rather like Ted, she is an optimist who chooses to remain stalwart and unshakable. Even when she is so busy that she has to "make time in my schedule to sit at my desk and cry," she carries on in her own style, on her own terms, supported by her friend Rebecca. For a while it is going as perfectly as her hairstyles, until a private and embarrassing video of Keeley is leaked on the internet, prompting the board of the venture capital company who funded her business to shut down KJPR. Without venture capital, Keeley's business is over.

And with that, the writers of the show lead us into a real world, often overlooked, mega-important problem for women—the lack of venture capital available for them. Lack of VC, as it is called, remains one of the most shocking examples of gender bias in the world. Fewer than 3 percent of female businesses receive VC, according to the *Harvard Business Review*. Yes, you read that right. Three percent! The rest of all VC—the kind that allowed companies like Meta (Facebook) and Google to grow to what they are today—goes to male-led businesses. This is because the predominantly male-led VC investment companies tend to invest in the companies that reflect what they know and feel most comfortable with—namely and pointedly, other men.

The statistics get a lot worse if you are a woman of color, and there is proof that if a woman includes a man's name in her application for funding, she is more likely to be considered. "We hear a lot about the gender pay gap.... But those gaps are dwarfed by the gap in funding for startups," says Julia Boorstin in her book *When Women Lead: What They Achieve, Why They Succeed and How We Can Learn from Them* (Avid Reader Press) in which she presents the shocking data about how hard it is for female entrepreneurs to get funding, but the miracles that happen when they do. "All those statistics are what make the women who have managed to raise financing and grow a business all the more remarkable," she says.

Given the stats, you could argue that the ease with which Keeley gets her initial VC for KJPR is not very realistic. But maybe that is the point. Maybe the writers are showing us a vision of what could be real if more women were given VC. There is now overwhelming evidence to show that the real-life female entrepreneurs who receive VC funding are super safe business bets.

Businesses started by women deliver higher revenues—more than twice as much per dollar invested – than those founded by men, according to a study commissioned by BCG, the Boston Consultancy Group ("Why Women-Owned Startups Are a Better Bet"). Teams composed entirely of female founders also sell or go public faster than all male teams, with higher valuations.

The point is when women are given the chance to show what they are capable of, they have proved themselves to be remarkable. As disheartening as some of the real-world facts and figures can be, there are some extraordinary stories of how difficult situations have been overcome. Over the last 100 years, women have become good at holding rallies, calling out inequity, and bringing attention to what needs to be done. We have even invented our own special day to celebrate ourselves: International Women's Day. Contrary to Hollywood's fixation with female rivalry, we are good at supporting each other and raising each other up. We just have to keep going. Being resilient lionesses who support each other is what has made the greatest gains so far.

When President Obama first took office at the White House in 2009, two thirds of the top aides he inherited were men. The women there were frequently overlooked and had to fight hard to get into important meetings. When they finally got a seat at the table, they often found that no one listened to what they had to say. Their voices were either ignored or the men in the room picked up on their ideas and claimed them as their own. It is a pattern that women in boardrooms around the world are familiar with.

So female staffers developed a meeting strategy that has become famous, called "amplification." When a woman made an important point in a meeting, another woman in the room would repeat it, amplifying it, and being sure to give credit to the woman who had said it.

If it still went ignored, another woman in the room would repeat it, once more giving credit to the source. It would continue for as many times as was required, with as many women as there were in the room, which ultimately forced the men to recognize the contribution and be unable to take credit themselves.

Testament to how clever a trick it was, women eventually gained parity with men in the President's inner circle. Their voices were finally heard, and the trick is often now passed between women across many business circles, often also referred to as Shine Theory.

Shine Theory works on the idea that it is better to support and befriend other women than compete with them. "It's an investment, over the long term, in helping someone be their best self—and relying on their help in return," explain US podcast hosts Ann Friedman and Aminatou Sow, who invented the term. "It is a conscious decision to bring your full self to your friendships, and to not let insecurity or envy ravage them.

"Shine Theory is a commitment to asking, 'Would we be better as collaborators than as competitors?' The answer is almost always yes. People know you by the company you keep. Shine Theory is recognizing that true confidence is infectious, and if someone is tearing you down or targeting you as competition, it's often because they are lacking in confidence or support themselves. It's a practice of cultivating a spirit of genuine happiness and excitement when your friends are doing well, and being there for them when they aren't."

Hard to imagine a more *Ted Lasso* theory than that.

INSPIRATION

"Champions keep playing until they get it right."

—Billie Jean King, former world no. 1 tennis player, advocate for gender equality who famously won the "Battle of the Sexes" tennis match in 1973 and argued that the prize money for professional female tennis players should be the same as for men

*"Don't think about making women fit the world—
think about making the world fit women."*

—Gloria Steinem, journalist, sociopolitical activist

"If your actions create a legacy that inspires others to dream more, learn more, do more and become more, then you are an excellent leader."

—Dolly Parton, singer-songwriter, philanthropist, and businesswoman

"Think like a queen. A queen is not afraid to fail. Failure is another steppingstone to greatness."

—Oprah Winfrey, talk show host, producer, actress, author, and media proprietor

"I raise up my voice—not so that I can shout, but so that those without a voice can be heard. … We cannot all succeed when half of us are held back."

—Malala Yousafzai, female education activist, author, speaker, and Nobel Peace Prize laureate

"I'd rather regret the risks that didn't work out than the chances I didn't take at all."

—Simone Biles, gymnast and Olympic gold medalist

"Women are like teabags. We don't know our true strength until we are in hot water."

—Eleanor Roosevelt, former First Lady of the United States from 1933 to 1945

"The beauty of being a feminist is that you get to be whatever you want. And that's the point."

—Shonda Rhimes, television producer, screenwriter, and founder of the production company Shondaland

"There is no limit to what we, as women, can accomplish."

—Michelle Obama, attorney, author, and former First Lady of the United States from 2009 to 2017

7
MOVE THE GOALPOSTS

"You say impossible, but all I hear is 'I'm possible.' "
—Ted Lasso

WHETHER YOU LIKE soccer or know nothing about it like Ted when he arrives in London, it is hard to imagine a more powerful example of women collectively overcoming odds than the 2023 Women's World Cup. It is one of the biggest global breakthrough stories of female empowerment this decade.

At the very end of the third season when the *Ted Lasso* story lines are being wrapped up, the writers give us a prescient nod to it when Keeley presents a white folder with KJPR on the cover to Rebecca. "I've got something to show you," she says, looking her confidently in the eye. She knows Rebecca is going to love her idea, and within minutes of opening the folder, the two women are screaming with joy.

The suggestion of an AFC Richmond Women's Team was perhaps always likely to turn up in *Ted Lasso*. There was a hint toward it in the first episode of the first season when Ted watches the schoolgirl, played by Shannon Hayes, single-handedly take on a group of boys on Richmond Green and dribbling the ball away from them, showing us that women can not only play soccer, sometimes they are better at it too. "Sometimes the best way to stick it to the man is to go right through his legs," Ted remarks to Coach Beard (played by Brendan Hunt).

Just as women were once not allowed to vote, or open bank accounts, or have a mortgage in their own name, women were once banned from playing professional soccer in England, Scotland, Wales, Ireland, Denmark, Belgium, Brazil, France, Norway, Nigeria, the Soviet Union, Spain, and Germany. Yes, you read that right! There was an actual ban on women kicking a ball around a field in any kind of professional league. What makes the story even more incredible is that the ban did not end in England until 1971!

Now fast forward to the Women's World Cup in 2023, when ticket sales and viewing figures broke all global records and women were finally seen in a cultural space they had long been denied. It was a triumphant showcase of what happens when women come together, when odds are beaten, when discrimination is fought against, when women are just given an equal chance. No disrespect to Spain, who won, but it almost did not matter who the winning team was because the real winners were women everywhere and young girls. All the players were champions in overcoming odds. More than any Women's World Cup before it (and it only began in 1991), 2023 was the year that showed future generations of girls how strong, competitive, and resilient women are.

In many ways, you might think the writers of *Ted Lasso* were oracles in suggesting an AFC Richmond Women's Team long before the Women's World Cup. But in July 2022, while the third season of *Ted Lasso* was being filmed in Richmond, England's National Women's Football Team, aptly better known as the Lionesses, was beating Germany in the UEFA Women's European Cup final at Wembley only a few miles away. That match also broke records, and stories of the Lionesses filled every newspaper, TV, and radio show. The girls' pictures stared back from packets of chips and soda cans everywhere—a moment that cannot have been lost on the show's writers.

So, since *Ted Lasso* is a show that is ostensibly about soccer, let's take a minute to look at the prospects for a real-life AFC Richmond Women's Team and the real-life history on which it would rest.

Before World War I, both men and women played organized soccer in England on a relatively equal playing field (forgive another pun). Given that England is recognized as the birthplace of soccer, this is relevant. The women's teams attracted huge crowds. Many of the matches raised money for charities. (Women like to work that way.) But the English Football Association saw the popularity of women's soccer as competition for the profits of the men's game, so in 1921 they deemed the game to be "unsuitable for females and not to be encouraged." The decision for the ban is believed to have been triggered by a 1920 women's match in Liverpool that attracted 53,000 spectators. Other countries soon instituted injunctions of their own.

When the ban was lifted fifty years later, the damage to women's soccer was catastrophic. Other countries lifted their bans with their own timelines, but the damage was everywhere. The sport had to restart again with no resources, no role models, and utterly stigmatized. None of the early team players who were brave enough to try to play soccer were full-time athletes. They had to train before and after they went to their jobs. They did not have enough uniforms and usually wore hand-me-downs from the men's teams. If they played in away matches, they frequently slept in sports gyms. They did not even have enough soccer balls, let alone pay. The ban had set in stone the idea that soccer was not a women's sport.

"In 1984 we were lucky enough to get to the UEFA Championship for Women," says Carol Thomas, who was captain of England's second-ever Women's National Team from 1976. "It was such a proud moment for us," she adds, though she could scarcely forget the disparity between how women's and men's teams were treated. "The men in the Football Association deemed—us being mere women—that we could only play for thirty-five minutes and with a size four football, so the game was in two legs.

"The first leg was in Sweden [whose team the English team was playing against]. Then we came back to London for the second leg. Several of the London clubs refused to put the game on for some reason. Luckily, Luton Town accepted us. But the pitch was absolutely atrocious. It had rained for two days, and the pitch was waterlogged." Today, the game would never have been played.

Carol is recognized today as one of the unsung pioneers of the women's game. She was inducted into the English Football Hall of Fame, and in 2022 she was awarded the British Empire Medal. Although she did receive some recognition during her time as England's captain, she has said that she has received the most media attention after the Lionesses won the UEFA Women's European Cup in 2022.

In every sense she was the perfect role model for girls and women—she proved herself over and over to be as tough as any man on the pitch, even more so because she was playing games without any of the support, pay, or luxury hotel rooms that her male counterparts were getting. But the problem was no one could see her unless you happened to go to one of the matches. You could not watch a women's match on television until 1989 in the United Kingdom (and even then, it was only once a year), so girls rarely if ever had the opportunity to see what Carol and her team were achieving. How can little girls dream of being professional soccer players when there are none to see?

The same story of underfunding and no role models has been played out in the United States and just about every other country around the world. It is why the current women players are extraordinary, the world over. It is why they understand that they are not just playing for themselves, they are playing for future generations.

"One of the most powerful things that we can do as players is exist in the public eye—just seeing women performing at the top level can help others believe that they can get there too," says Leah Williamson, who was responsible for leading the Lionesses, England's team, to UEFA Cup victory in 2022. She is now an advocate for girls playing soccer and author of *You Have the Power: Find Your Strength and Believe You Can* (Pan Macmillan).

"These girls are not the princesses that used to grace your bedtime stories. They are the warriors of today that had a voice when there was no say or sway. They rewrite the definition of strength year on year and know they are their own biggest competition. Tomorrow to them sounds like an opportunity."

Leah joined her first team as the only girl on a boys' team because there was no girls' team for her to join, a familiar story for many female players. Leah often credits her mother's encouragement for getting her into soccer. "I only played boys' football for a year, which was eventful, to say the least," she says.

"At the end of a game, a boy would be crying, and the parents would be saying, 'I can't believe you let a girl beat you.' It's not normally the boys, it's normally the parents that are uncomfortable with a girl being so good. That year was an eye-opener for me. There were parents screaming to their kids, 'Get the girl.' Occasionally, you know, I'd get a kid that would be riled up by his parents that would then try and snap my legs, basically."

After their win, England's Lionesses launched a campaign with an open letter to the British government calling on them to invest in girls' soccer in schools and ensure that girls are offered equal chances to play it at school. In 2023, Prime Minister Rishi Sunak finally announced measures to make that happen.

That fight for equality is happening all over the world. In the United States, the women's national soccer team has been relentless in working to close the pay gap between professional male soccer players and female professional players in their country. Women soccer players globally earn on average 25 cents for every dollar that their male soccer playing counterparts earn at a World Cup, according to a CNN study. A comparison of the big-name soccer stars' earnings shows an even greater disparity.

But in May 2022, the US women's team's long-fought dispute with the US Soccer Federation reached a settlement that guaranteed the women's and men's national teams equal pay in terms of salary, appearance fees, performance bonuses, and commercial revenue. There was also an agreement for the men's and women's teams to pool their World Cup prize money, which meant that although the US women's team was knocked out in the sixteenth round of the 2023 World Cup by Sweden, they still brought home their biggest payout ever, setting an example for the rest of the world. Other countries are now fighting for the same arrangement.

The 2023 Women's World Cup unleashed dozens of tales about remarkable women, all disproving the stereotyped perception of women being too fragile, or emotional, or in some way unequal to play. There were hundreds of stories of girls who had proved themselves initially on boys' teams because there were no girls' teams to join; and girls who had learned to play on improvised soccer pitches with improvised balls like Brazil's Marta Vieira da Silver, now considered one of the greatest female soccer players of all time who made her own soccer balls out of wadded plastic bags because she had no soccer ball to play with.

There is also the story of Nadia Nadim, a refugee from Afghanistan who fled to Denmark on the back of a truck after her father was murdered by the Taliban. Nadia trained to play soccer at the same time that she was studying for medical school. She has represented Denmark more than a hundred times, scored more than 225 goals, speaks eleven languages, and is now a doctor.

So, what might the prospects be for a real-life AFC Richmond women's team? Getting better all the time.

INSPIRATION FROM WOMEN IN SOCCER

"Real change lies within all of us. It is in the choices we make every day. It's in how we talk, who we hire, and what we permit others to say in our presence. It's in reading more, thinking more, considering a different perspective. At its simplest, it's in whether we're willing to spend even five minutes a day thinking about how we can make the world better."

—Megan Rapinoe, former captain of US Women's National Soccer Team

"By the time I was 22, I'd already had six major ankle injuries. But I haven't let this stop me. It's meant that I've had to work harder."

—Leah Williamson, captain of England's National Women's Team, otherwise known as the Lionesses

"My message to girls everywhere in this world: believe in yourself and trust yourself, because if you don't believe in yourself, no one else will."

— Marta Vieira da Silver, Brazilian player and United Nations Goodwill Ambassador

"The key is to just keep going. It's about having the resilience and perspective that not everything will go your way, but this doesn't mean it's catastrophic."

—Sam Kerr, captain of Australia's National Women's Team, otherwise known as the Matildas

"Always work hard, never give up, and fight until the end because it's never really over until the whistle blows."

—Alex Morgan, player for the US Women's National Soccer Team

"We need more women coaches. I think a lot of work has been done and is still necessary to do to get more females involved and to give opportunities and to take opportunities."

—Sarina Wiegman, coach for England's National Women's Team, otherwise known as the Lionesses

"It's not my place to evaluate communication practices or integrity, but I am sure that as world champions we do not deserve a culture so manipulative, hostile and controlling."

—Jenni Hemoso, player for Spain's National Women's Team in 2023 World Cup, who was grabbed by the country's FA president Luis Rubialies, kissed without her consent, and then pressured to drop her complaint

8

BELIEVE IN YOU

"I believe in believe."

—Ted Lasso

"DON'T SELL YOURSELF short. If anything, sell yourself tall and get it altered later," Ted says to Roy in the third season. We laugh, as we always do at Ted's humor, but there is wisdom in his words.

Ted Lasso is all about believing in ourselves. From his famous "Believe" sign that he tapes up on AFC Richmond's locker room wall to his motivational speeches telling us to not stress over the wins and losses but be our best selves, he is a living masterclass in encouraging confidence. It works like a dream for AFC Richmond.

But believing in ourselves is not always easy. How many of us sell ourselves short, not believing in what we're capable of? How many of us imagine we are not worthy? How many of us underestimate ourselves?

Both genders can struggle with lack of confidence. But women, it turns out, struggle with it more. A 2003 study carried out by Cornell University psychologist David Dunning and Washington State University psychologist Joyce Ehrlinger quantified this with a series of long-term tests looking into the relationship between confidence and competence. Their studies confirmed that men typically overestimate their abilities and performance, while women almost always underestimate both. What makes the study particularly relevant is that the actual performance of the men and the women did not differ at all. In other words, despite being equally capable, women tend to think they are not competent enough and this stops them from going after the things they want.

Confidence, that belief that we can succeed, is an elusive, hard to define quality that some people seem to have in bucketloads, and others not at all. At any social occasion, boardroom, school, or workplace, there will always be those who seem to exude a fearless can-do attitude and others who scarcely dare speak. But believing that we will succeed is a reliable predictor that we will. It is that simple. With confidence, you can do anything, but without it, you cannot even get the window table at A Taste of Athens, like Nate.

The good news is confidence, or self-efficacy as psychologists call it, can grow. It is not fixed or static. Part of self-confidence owes itself to genetics, how we are raised, and environmental factors, according to several studies conducted by Robert Plomin, professor of behavioral genetics at King's College London. But part of it also comes from choice and our own determination to increase it. Scientists talk about plasticity in our brains, an ability to mold or adapt its structure. Our plasticity allows us to become more confident if we are prepared to work at it.

This seems like an excellent moment to bring up Rebecca's secret confidence-boosting trick. Keeley brings Nate into Rebecca's office because he has told her he cannot get the window table he wants at his favorite restaurant because he is so lacking in confidence. Keeley wants Rebecca, who is obviously the doyenne of self-assertion, to show him how. You just need to be commanding, Rebecca tells him, to which Nate replies: "With the greatest respect, it's different for me, Ms. Welton. You command every room you walk into."

"Hardly," Rebecca replies. "Have you ever been in a room of football club chairmen? Every time I walk into one of those meetings, they look at me like some schoolgirl with pigtails. But I have a secret: I make myself big. Before I go into a room, I find somewhere private, I stand up on my tiptoes, put my arms in the air and make myself as big as possible to find my own power." She gives a demonstration so breathtakingly impressive that Nate and Keeley are at a loss for words, and we are in no doubt of its effectiveness. "It's a bit silly, but it works for me," she finishes up. "Find your own thing."

As hokey as it might seem, there is evidence to suggest that confidence-boosting tricks like making ourselves tall, sticking up a "Believe" sign, saying positive affirmations and listening to motivational speeches can make a difference. Remember how Colin Hughes (played by Billy Harris) kept telling himself: "I am a strong and capable man. I am not a piece of shit." For many people, positive affirmations can really help overcome self-doubt, fear, and self-sabotage. They are not a magic fix, but they can help contribute to getting past or ignoring the negative voices, thoughts, and fears inside our own heads.

We all hear negative thoughts inside our heads from time to time. The trick is to stop them from spiraling so that we end up talking ourselves out of doing the things we need to do to achieve our dreams. "We've gotten so used to our negative knee-jerk reactions to ourselves that we never think to question them," explains Jen Sincero, success coach and author of the bestseller *You Are a Badass: How to Stop Doubting your Greatness and Start Living an Awesome Life* (Hodder & Stoughton). "But once we become aware of our thought patterns and behaviors, we can consciously change them."

Getting outside of our comfort zones, taking action, and doing what we are most nervous of doing is where our confidence can really start to grow, according to Katty Kay and Claire Shipman, two TV reporters and political commentators who set out to explore the elusive nature of female confidence for their 2014 best-seller *The Confidence Code: The Science and Art of Self-Assurance—What Women Should Know* (HarperCollins), updated in 2018.

"Imagine all the things over the years you wish you had said or done or tried—but didn't because something held you back," explain Kay and Shipman, who interviewed hundreds of women in senior roles, as well as neurologists, psychologists, and coaches for their book. "Whether you work or you don't, whether you want the top job or the part-time job—wouldn't it just be great to slough off the anxiety and the fretting about all the things you'd love to try but don't trust yourself to do? In the most basic terms, what we need to do is start acting and risking and failing; and stop mumbling and apologizing and prevaricating. It isn't that women don't have the ability to succeed; it's that we don't seem to believe we *can* succeed, and that stops us from even trying."

Our lack of faith in our abilities goes all the way to boardrooms and corridors of power, according to Kay and Shipman, who found that even senators and other women in government, for all that they had achieved, still admitted to lacking confidence at certain times and feeling like imposters. "Woman after woman, from lawmakers to CEOs, expressed to us some version of the same inexplicable feeling that they don't fully own their right to rule at the top," say Kay and Shipman. "Too many of the fantastically capable women we met and spoke with seemed to lack a firm faith in their abilities."

Among those that they interviewed was Christine Lagarde, the first female managing director of the International Monetary Fund, a very powerful woman at the top of her game. "I would often get nervous about presentations and speaking," she told Kay and Shipman. "There were moments when I had to screw up my courage to raise my hand or make a point, rather than hanging back… There were moments where I had to sort of go deep inside myself and pull [out] my self-confidence, background, history, experience, and all the rest of it, to assert a particular point."

Seventy-five percent of female executives across different industries were found to experience imposter syndrome during their careers, according to a 2023 study by the multinational professional services network KPMG. Imposter syndrome, a term developed by psychologists to describe high achievers who believe themselves to be less intelligent or capable, regardless of their professional or academic accomplishments, can affect both genders. But it is women who feel its burden the most, according to the study.

It makes sense, given history. For years, women have been denied access to senior workplace positions, watched men less qualified than themselves be promoted while they were passed over. They have been shut out of cultural spaces, workspaces, and sports spaces, and faced professional and domestic barriers at every turn, repeatedly being told they were not good enough. That would knock anyone's confidence.

The solution is to remind ourselves of that history and work on changing it. As a society, we need more women in senior positions so that women like Rebecca are not the only ones in rooms full of men, and subsequent generations can see that. And as individuals we have to keep challenging ourselves to try new things because that is how our confidence will grow.

Confidence grows from taking risks, according to

Kay and Shipman. If we fail, it does not matter. If we are not perfect, it does not matter. Both fear of failure and an insistence on perfection stop us from even trying. The key point is to stop overthinking whether we should or should not do something, but just do it. And believe in ourselves.

CONFIDENCE-BOOSTING TRICKS FROM THE SHOW

1. Go buy yourself a "Believe" sign. It reflects the belief in possibility and reminds us to have faith in ourselves. Ted says he has the same sign pasted all over his house, including on the bathroom mirror, so he sees it first thing in the morning and last thing at night when he rationalizes being too tired to floss.
2. Repeat after Colin: "I am strong and capable."
3. Challenge yourself. "Are we nuts for doing this?" Ted asks Coach Beard on the plane heading to the UK to take up his new job as coach for Richmond. It is a flicker of self-doubt. But then he reminds himself: "Takin' on a challenge is a lot like riding a horse. If you're comfortable while you're doin' it, you're probably doin' it wrong."

4. Do as Rebecca does: "Before I go into a room, I find somewhere private, I stand up on my tiptoes, put my arms in the air and make myself as big as possible to find my own power."
5. Give yourself some secret confidence-boosting initials. On the pinball machine at The Crown and Anchor, Dr. Sharon signs her name as SMF. Ted tries to guess what it stands for. The answer, she tells him, is Sexy Mother F***er.
6. Make good choices. "Every choice is a chance. It's our choices that show us who we truly are," says Ted.
7. Dream big. "You might never wake up," says soccer legend Zava.

9

BE TRUE TO YOU

"Coach, I'm me. Why would I want to be anything else?"
—Jamie Tartt

AT AN AGE when many Hollywood actresses see their careers diminish and at a height of five foot eleven, against which most male lead actors do not care to stand next to for long, single mom Hannah Waddingham's personal story is living proof that the odds are not always unsurmountable and sometimes you just have to keep believing in yourself.

Her story is every bit as inspirational for women as the character she plays, so just for a moment, let's find a little encouragement from the lives of the actors who play our TV favorites—each of them unique, fabulous women who are familiar with overcoming a few odds, but know the importance of trusting in themselves.

"The thing for me has always been Ted's line when

he is in the locker room and he just goes 'Onward, forward,' " Hannah explains. "I love that because you need to move forward from the bad times, but also not get caught up in yourself in the good times. So onward, forward, always," she says.

Hannah was forty-five years old when she was cast as Rebecca. Although she had been a working actor and singer all her life, she was not particularly well known, certainly not in the international arena. Her age and height put her among the many actresses that Hollywood and the entertainment industry typically ignore. "Being a woman who's not small, very tall, I'd always struggled," she says. "The number of times they'd be like 'We've already cast the guy, who's five feet seven.' Whereas when I went in for this, Jason was like 'I don't care if she wears four-inch heels. Let's do it.' It was so nice. I was forty-five when we started shooting, which in itself is unusual—ridiculous that it's unusual—and Jason was like 'I don't care.' That is a completely unique situation to find yourself in."

Imposing, statuesque, and always a straight shooter in the way she talks, Hannah commands an attitude that is every inch as powerful as the one her character plays, which explains why so many women are fans. She seems to be fearless, the kind of woman you'd want to have as your best friend—deeply loyal to those around her, who would have your back. She also has a notable lack of vanity. It was, in fact, Hannah who wanted Rebecca to be the same age as her in real life, to make her story more authentic. In every sense, she is a lioness.

She grew up in Wandsworth, South London, and often spent her school vacations watching her mother rehearse at London's Coliseum, home to England's National Opera, where she sang in the chorus. Hannah's mother and her grandmother were both opera singers, and her father is a retired marketing director. "My life was sitting in the stalls, watching the greats, like Lesley Garrett, Bryn Terfel," says Waddingham. "This extraordinary music falling on my ears. But there was nothing la-di-da about us, we were a grounded, normal family—we saw how hard Mom worked. I remember thinking, 'If your job isn't singing or dancing, what do you do?' I never had a plan B—not in an arrogant way, but that was my vocation."

After graduating from London's Academy of Live and Recorded Arts, Hannah began her career performing in dinner theater, which ultimately led to West End and Broadway musicals, like *Spamalot, Kiss Me Kate,* and *The Wizard of Oz.* Television and film work followed with roles in Disney's *Hocus Pocus 2, Game of Thrones,* and *Sex Education.* But it was her role as Rebecca that has sent her career soaring, winning her an Emmy for Outstanding Supporting Actress in a Comedy Series. "This is happy times for a little girl from South London," she says simply, ever grateful to the opportunity she was given.

"From the moment I auditioned for Rebecca, I just felt her ripple through me. I knew who she was—I knew her acerbic bark, her dry wit, the way she'd suffered controlling, verbal abuse from a partner. I've been through that myself, so playing her brought me great catharsis. She's in her forties, divorced, a very wealthy woman who appears to have it all together but really doesn't know where she's going in life. I wanted to be very delicate in honoring that. I feel a huge responsibility to serve her and all those women and men in their forties because it's not easy finding yourself at that age on the heap, and that's what she's doing, trying to keep her head above water."

Hannah has never hidden that she knows personally what it is like to walk away from a destructive relationship and be single in her forties. Like Rebecca who is told she cannot have children in the third season, Hannah also experienced that heart-breaking moment in real life, although that information turned out to be wrong and she has a daughter, Kitty, whom she raises as a single mom—a situation we know is not easy.

Playing Rebecca in *Ted Lasso* was the role she had never given up hope in finding, particularly since it also happened to be filmed in Richmond, very close to where she lived. Any farther away and she would have been forced to turn it down because she needed to be near her daughter, who had once fallen seriously sick with a rare auto-immune episode while Hannah was away filming. Hannah had vowed she would never work that far away from her again. So, at the *Ted Lasso* auditions she found herself asking Jason: "Where's this going to shoot?"

"Jason said, 'Richmond, ma'am,' " explains Hannah. "I said to him: 'Richmond, Virginia?' He said: 'Er, no, Richmond, Surrey.' It was twenty minutes' drive from my house, past deer in Richmond Park. The bit was between my teeth. I was like, 'I'm having this part!' "

Arriving during the pandemic years, *Ted Lasso* has

often been credited for being what the world needed at the time. "Chicken soup for our souls," Hannah calls it. "I was thrilled when the show became such a success because it was celebrating kindness and being funny rather than just roasting everyone and being snippy and bitchy, you know? It was a reminder that you don't have to be cutting to be funny."

What no one could have predicted was how she and Juno Temple would become best friends in real life, both describing their friendship with each other as a treasured gift. "Off set we are just in love with each other," says Hannah. "She [Juno] is one of the great loves of my life. It was just effortless from day one and it's got deeper and deeper ever since."

Fun, bright, and with a wicked sense of humor, Juno has her own story of courage and resilience. She already had a rising career with parts in *Atonement, Notes on a Scandal, Killer Joe, Maleficent,* and *Unsane,* when *Ted Lasso* came along. But she had never worked in comedy before and was so uncertain of herself as a comedic actress that when Jason Sudeikis texted her asking her to read for the part, she assumed he had texted the wrong person. "I was sure he'd texted the wrong actress," she says.

She had to trust herself, have faith in her own abilities, and be true to what she was capable of to play Keeley. That must have taken some fearlessness. "Whenever I was panicking, Jason was like, 'You're okay. You got it.' " And of course, she had. Overcoming our own nerves is 100 percent a lioness move.

Like Hannah, Juno was born in London, later

moving to Taunton, Somerset, and had the creative arts as her childhood backdrop. Her father is the film director Julien Temple, her mother is the producer Amanda Pirie, and she landed her first film role at the age of seven in the 1997 film *Vigo: Passion for Life*. Acting was in her blood. "I was constantly learning about all different lives and all different people and all different rhythms," she recalls of her childhood. "I didn't actually go to university, so I feel like every time I do a job, it's like a tiny little university experience for me."

Juno talks about *Ted Lasso* as saving her life. "It's been a really important experience for me.... And the feedback that I've had from people that have watched the show, talking about the joy it's brought them, I mean, I don't know if this will ever happen in my career again, but honestly, this show saved my life too."

One of the moments that Juno cherishes is when a fan told her and Hannah that she was showing *Ted Lasso* to her daughter because she wanted her to see the female empowerment that happens when two women really support each other.

Becoming best friends with Hannah is, of course, also part of that story. Juno recalls meeting Hannah in the restroom minutes before the first *Ted Lasso* table read in 2019: "We were two women walking into a room with a lot of very handsome, very talented gentlemen," she says. "I mean, *very* handsome and *very* talented. So, I think having a momentary check-in with another woman in a ladies' loo is kind of the best place to start a friendship like that."

Juno says she was in awe of Hannah in their first scene together.

"I remember the lion and panda moment where Keeley is watching Rebecca and thinking, 'That is just such a great speech. I would love to be able to give a speech like that.' But then it was also Juno watching Hannah. I just remember thinking, 'I would like to be able to give a great speech like that.'… We found each other so easily in real life that it meant that we could lend that to our ladies that we played. Hannah's become one of the most important females to ever enter my life," she says. "It's been amazing to go through this with her."

Seeing Hannah succeed as an older actress was also inspirational for her. "You do spend a lot of time being around people that panic about aging because you're just like, 'Oh God, I'm going to pass my sell-by date at any minute.'" Juno turned thirty while filming the first season, but Hannah made her rethink her approach to growing older in the TV and film industry. "We forget that actually, as women, we grow more and more comfortable in our bodies and in our existence as we get older—and we care less about the exterior presentation and more about the interior presentation."

Besides Hannah and Juno, there is another brave, fearless woman in *Ted Lasso* that this book would be incomplete without. In the second season, Sarah Niles, who plays sports psychologist Dr. Sharon Fieldstone, joins the cast. Like Hannah, Sarah was in her forties and had been a working actor all her life but had not achieved an international level of fame. In an industry that is notoriously ageist, and where lead roles for women of color are scarce, Sarah was all too familiar with having to be tenacious. Representation of Black talent in film and television remains disturbingly unequal, with Black actors playing only 11 percent of leading film roles, according to a recent McKinsey report.

Like Juno, Sarah was a little nervous when she first arrived on set. The show was already well-established. Everyone knew each other already. And she was keen to find the right mix between kindness and professionalism for the sports psychologist she plays. "A lot of it was trusting in me, myself…stepping out of my own way," she explains.

It was important for Sarah that Dr. Sharon was a strong woman. "A lot of Black women, especially in America, love Dr. Sharon because she's standing in her power and her strength," she says. "It's about seeing yourself represented. Often when you see Black female characters on screen, they're going through some kind of turmoil. Dr. Sharon just exists in her power. I've learned a lot from playing her."

It was also important to Sarah that she was vulnerable. Jason Sudeikis had recommended that Sarah read some of Brené Brown's books when it came to researching her role. "I think vulnerability is such a powerful thing that we're always told not to be," Sarah explains. "We're told to always be strong, and success, success, success. But I think Ted and Dr. Sharon teach each other that's it's okay to be vulnerable."

She is referring, of course, to the scenes where she

is knocked off her bicycle and ends up in the hospital. Ted comes to offer help but she does not want to accept. Like Ted she had put walls around herself to project her professional self, but when she eventually tells him that she was scared when she was knocked off her bike, she finds a deeper, more significant strength. "Thanks to you, I've learned that expressing my vulnerabilities can help my patients with theirs," she says to Ted. "You helped me become a better therapist. And that's saying something because I was already f***ing brilliant."

Sarah had always flitted between the theater and screen, a regular performer at the UK's revered National Theatre and Royal Shakespeare Company, and also roles in British television including *Doctor Who, I May Destroy You*, and *Catastrophe. Ted Lasso* changed everything for her, especially when she was nominated for an Emmy for her role.

"My mom and my dad are so thrilled. They come from the Caribbean… They never did jobs that were meant for them to enjoy," she says. "And here I am, doing a joyous job that I absolutely love… I don't know many people who come from my background, from the UK, who get a nomination like that. It means that people have seen that character, and she's had an impact, enough to warrant me being nominated. That means so much to me."

BUILD YOUR LIONESS STRENGTHS

1. Trust who you are. Inspiration is useful, but never abandon authenticity.
2. Even when the odds are stacked against you, keep going.
3. Find the other woman in the room and make her your friend.
4. Show vulnerability. It is not a weakness, it is strength.
5. Practice humility. Remain positive. If necessary, watch *Ted Lasso* over again.
6. "*Listen to your gut. And on your way down to your gut, check in with your heart. Between those two things, they'll let you know what's what.*"—Ted Lasso

10

BE KIND

Gradarius Firmus Victoria.

IN A SHOW that has so much forgiveness at its heart, you have to look hard to find the villain in *Ted Lasso*. For a brief second, we might have thought it was Rebecca because she was so intent on revenge at the start. We might have thought it was kitman Nate Shelley, who tore up Ted's "Believe" sign.

But in the end, the person who never seeks redemption, but needs to, is the contact in Rebecca's phone who is listed as "The Devil," her ex-husband, Rupert Mannion. In the series finale, his cruel misogyny gets its comeuppance, confirming, just in case there was ever any doubt, that the show had feminism embedded in its DNA all along.

The female solidarity in this show is so real you could build walls with it. Remember Rebecca's father's funeral, when Sassy (played by Ellie Taylor), her old school friend, meets Rupert at the back of the church? Loyal, razor-sharp, and true to her name, she cannot resist taking Rupert down when he tells her he is a changed man because he has a daughter now.

"Oh, right. Having a daughter erases all the shitty things you've done to women in your lifetime," she says smiling hard as she relishes the moment. Given that Rupert is the man who claimed he didn't want children and then just as Rebecca reached the age when having children was impossible, had a baby with another woman, we are cheering Sassy on. Of course we are. We are with Sassy all the way on this.

We are cheering even louder at the end of the third season when Rupert has been hit by unsavory allegations of sexual impropriety and is about to be ousted from his position as CEO of West Ham, the club he bought, having lost AFC Richmond in his divorce settlement to Rebecca. The MeToo movement storms into the world of *Ted Lasso* with an army of women cheering.

"Heard the news. Ouch!" Sassy gloats when she bumps into Rupert again before the last match of the season, West Ham against AFC Richmond. "Looks like you're going to lose another team. My God, you get through them like wives, or mistresses, or I'm assuming tubes of hemorrhoid cream."

The MeToo movement showed us the power of women coming together. Tarana Burke's original "MeToo" campaign, launched in 2007, aimed to provide support to survivors of sexual violence who were marginalized, underrepresented, and without a community to protect them. By 2017, it had been relaunched and became a tipping point in history when the Hollywood movie mogul Harvey Weinstein was exposed as a sexual predator.

More than eighty women in the movie industry accused Weinstein of rape, assault, or sexual harassment, his arrival in the news prompting the actor Alyssa Milano to write on social media: "If all the women who have been sexually harassed or assaulted wrote 'Me too' as a status, we might give people a sense of the magnitude of the problem."

And they did just that—by the millions. It was not just one man who thought he could use his power to assault and control women, it was many. Women who had been silenced or frightened to speak out found their voice and the power structures previously used to protect harassers crumbled. Many high-profile men, to whom Rupert Mannion shows a striking resemblance, found their careers at a sudden dead end and the conversation about men's behavior toward women moved to the center stage.

Since then, the movement has had its critics, not just from angry male commentators, but also some feminists who argue that the grouping of such a wide spectrum of sexual misbehavior has lost a sense of nuance. Others argue that the course correction has gone too far with men backed into a corner, fearful of saying or doing anything that could be misinterpreted. Many believe that the movement now looks like a vindictive plot against men, while others maintain that until there is no sexual violence or harassment against women, it has not gone far enough.

In a polarized world, it has become more controversial than Roy's rainbow-colored tie-dye T-shirt, but there is no denying that the movement has changed the landscape and demonstrated the collective power of women. Collective support is where it is at. But while female solidarity gives women clout and that warm, fuzzy feeling of not being alone, it has never been, nor ought to be about man-hating. And that is where *Ted Lasso* strikes a clever and careful balance reminding us that men have their issues too.

There is a subtle touch to that grand finale scene when AFC Richmond is playing West Ham. After pushing his own coach to the ground, Rupert has the whole stadium calling him a "wanker" (British term for "jerk," but more offensive). Sassy, in the stands next to Rebecca, cannot resist joining in with the chant, but Rebecca is not calling Rupert names at all. She looks sorry for him. There is genuine pity and concern for him in her eyes.

Maybe, in that moment, the writers of *Ted Lasso* were subtly drawing our attention to the complexity of it all. Like Ted says, "humans contain multitudes," a reference to a Walt Whitman poem. The point is that feminism was never about hating men. It was and remains about equality.

"Until now, feminism has worked on making women equal to men in power, safety, status, politics, relationships, and the economy. But it now urgently needs to embark on the second phase—which is absolutely predicted by the word 'equality,' " says feminist author Caitlin Moran in her book *What About Men?* (Ebury Press).

Although no one is suggesting that we need to sympathize too hard with Rupert Mannion and sexual predators like him, the reality is that the patriarchy hurts men as much as it hurts women. Men make up the majority of gang members, the homeless, the unemployed, the murdered, the prison population, and of addicts. Most awful of all, they also make up the majority of suicides, a subject that *Ted Lasso* brings into focus in the second season when we learn that Ted's dad committed suicide.

Toxic masculinity, lack of mental health resources, and the difficulties men have in talking about their problems to each other, or anyone at all, conspire to hurt men as much as they do women. That is a theme of the show that resonated so loud, it took Jason Sudeikis and some of the other writers and actors to the White House as part of the President's efforts to raise mental health awareness. And it is a mega, mega (keep saying "mega") important point.

"Woman up!" Ted tells Jamie Tartt (Phil Dunster) in the second season.

"I think you mean 'Man up,'" Jamie says.

Coach Beard and Ted shake their heads. "You've been manning up for a while now and look where that's got you."

The societal expectation that men need to be tough, macho, and anti-women if they are to be real men is a trope that hurts everyone. Studies investigating attitudes concerning masculinity found that men who had stereotypical views were less likely to seek mental health services and more likely to take greater risks with their health ("An Investigation of Attitudes toward Psychological Help-Seeking," by Omar Yousaf Ph.D. 2015).

Male suicide—rates are three and a half times higher for men than women—is so pervasive that the American Psychological Association published guidelines to help psychologists work with men in 2019. Drawing on more than forty years of research, they wrote that traditional masculinity—marked out by stoicism, competitiveness, dominance, and aggression—is psychologically harmful.

"What men and boys need is feminism," argues Moran, who has built a career around her feminist books and views. "What women need is boys and men who use feminism. Feminism is still the only thing we've invented that exists solely to look at the problems of gender, and bring about equality between the sexes."

Prior to writing *What About Men?*, Moran was at a speaking event when she was asked by the mother of teenage boys: "Do you have any advice for men?" When Moran kept being asked the same question at events, she began her research, only to find that men and boys, particularly straight men, were struggling, feeling alienated and uncertain of their place in a new feminist world, but unlike women who find it so much easier to show their fears and support each other, the men were internalizing and lonely. "I think my presumption—as a forty-eight year-old, fourth-wave feminist—was that straight white men were generally doing so fine that they were the one sociodemographic group you could lovingly beat up on a bit."

Struck by an unexpected guilt, she wrote *What About Men?* in an attempt to highlight some of the difficulties men face and encourage more love and understanding between the genders. "Being honest, breaking taboos, starting conversations, organizing campaigns, forming alliances, and supporting each other. These are the basic feminist tools women have used to improve their lives immeasurably in the last two hundred years." Now men need to use the same tools to solve their own problems.

Arguably, that might have been the intention behind *Ted Lasso* all along—or at least in part. It created a funny, kind, inclusive open arena where men were given the space to unbutton their masculinity, a world where a team of macho sportsmen were allowed to cry in rom-coms, embrace a gay team member, and support each other without it feeling forced or out of the ordinary.

It was a world that somehow redressed the male–female balance where a powerful female boss was respected, and an all-male team was given permission to be themselves and to let macho pretenses dissolve away. The Diamond Dogs, Ted's emotional support group, is essentially *Ted Lasso*'s entire ethos in microcosm—a venue where men are happy to become vulnerable in front of each other and everyone howls after achieving emotional breakthroughs. That is feminism for men.

Ted Lasso was never really about soccer. It was about generosity, life's boundlessness, the vibrancy of equality and, above all, the miraculous capacity we have within us for change. It was Mary Poppins arriving and then disappearing having worked a kind of magic, leaving a legacy of trickle-down kindness and compassion for lions *and* lionesses.

A NOTE FROM THE AUTHOR

MY TED LASSO STORY:
How Ted Lasso Changed My Life

NOT LONG AFTER the first season of *Ted Lasso* began on Apple TV+, a car accidentally scraped the side of my Subaru in a parking lot. Ordinarily, there might have been some expletives. There was a pandemic on. I was on edge.

But *Ted Lasso* oddly came into my head in that moment, and unexpectedly, I found myself wondering what he might do in this precise circumstance. Like everyone, I'd been moved by the warmth of the show and knew that Ted would react generously instead of angrily. Nothing could be done about the scrape on the side of my car, so why get hot under the collar about it? "Big whoop," I could hear Ted say. So, going against my worst instincts, I was generous to the other driver, not angry, just like Ted would have been. And crazy as it seems, as I drove home, I felt good about myself. I had an annoying scrape down the side of my car, but I was smiling more than the hour before when I didn't have it there. That sent me down a research path—not just to car body repair shops—but into psychology. I am a journalist. Research is what I do. If a sitcom on TV could affect me that way, maybe there was more to it. Maybe it was affecting others too.

I discovered that many of the storylines in *Ted Lasso* owe themselves to what is known as the positive psychology movement. The trick that I had fallen upon in a parking lot, choosing how to react in an adverse situation, was written about by psychologist Viktor E. Frankl in his book *Man's Search for Meaning* (Beacon Press). Based on his own experience in a World War II concentration camp, he argued that if we approach difficulties with a more optimistic, hopeful frame of mind, we can shape our own reality.

All those tactics that we see Ted use, from his curiosity of others to his "Believe" sign, from his forgiveness of adversaries to his respect for everyone, are rooted in positive psychology that many people, better qualified than me, believe can boost happiness and well-being.

I couldn't help but wonder if there was a book to be written about it. My career was stuttering along like an old car. (The internet has not been kind to journalists.) So I pitched the idea of *What Would Ted Lasso Do? How Ted's Positive Approach Can Help You* to two book publishers, and when the CEO of one of them came back to me within two days, and the other within a week, I knew I was onto something.

The problem was, by then we were all waiting for the

third season of the show, and we didn't know when Apple TV+ was going to release it. Traditionally published books take a while to find their way into bookshops, and the publishers were concerned that the third season of Ted Lasso might come and go before the book made it to the stores. "Of course, you could publish it yourself quicker than I could," one of the CEOs said to me.

Who, me? I had absolutely no idea how to self-publish a book, let alone market it. He was out of his mind. No way.

One of the great things about having a reputable publisher back a book you have written is their endorsement of it. You get editors who believe it is worthwhile. I'd had two books published traditionally before, so I knew that feeling, which is as reassuring as *Ted Lasso* himself.

Self-publishing is a whole different ballgame. It requires a lot more self-belief. You are on your own. No endorsement from anyone other than your husband, your bestie, and the dog. There is just this hope that maybe your idea is halfway decent, that maybe someone might get something out of reading it, and maybe you are not crazy after all. And all the time, there is a voice inside your head telling you that what you have written is not good enough, *you* are not good enough. (That is imposter syndrome right there.) "Give up on the idea and don't take the risk," says the voice.

It became a moment to test out the theory behind the very title I was pitching. *What Would Ted Lasso Do?* By then, of course, all that positive psychology, those Lassoisms, and power of believing was running amok inside my head. I had rewatched the show several times. Why not "Believe" like Ted Lasso seemed to be telling me? If you are going to write it, you have to believe it yourself, right?

So I stuck a "Believe" sign up in my office and embarked on self-publishing, reminding myself at every setback along the way that "taking on a challenge is a lot like riding a horse. If you're comfortable while you're doing it, you're probably doing it wrong."

And there were many setbacks. A so-called editor disappeared with my $600 without making a single edit only weeks before the publishing date. My computer imploded, taking with it several chapters, also only weeks before the publishing date. I discovered that proofreading is just not a skill I own (apologies to all those who bought the early copies with typos). I also recall bursting into tears when all the pre-sales I thought I had gained on Amazon disappeared (although I did find them later). I might have reacted well to a scrape along the side of a car, but I cannot say I did as well in my endeavors to self-publish.

But I did keep going. *Ted Lasso's* optimism really did ring in my ears. I believed I could do it. And most astonishing of all, a whole lot of people—more than I ever imagined—were kind enough to buy the book. It is an Amazon bestseller, has won an Indie Book of the Year Award, and the reviews have been kinder than I ever expected. I cannot begin to say how appreciative I am of that. People have written to tell me what the book has meant to them, how it kept *Ted Lasso* alive for them, which has become an important part of my *Ted Lasso* journey.

Many people also shared with me that their lives had been improved by *Ted Lasso*. It was not just me who had felt its positivity. When the show first came out, the world was hurting. A global pandemic was tearing through our lives, upending families, destroying businesses, and isolating us. In my research, I spoke to many who found personal strength through Ted's messaging. British actor Emmy McMorrow left a challenging relationship and started a new business after watching the show. "Ted gave me confidence in myself when I really needed it," says Emmy, who runs Ted Lasso Tours around Richmond, which if you are a fan of the show, you will not want to miss.

Others had similar experiences. Marita Barth lost a family member during the pandemic but found friendship in co-hosting the popular podcast about the books in *Ted Lasso* called Coach Beard's Book Club. Sports psychologist Dr Yori launched a *Ted Lasso* community Twitter account entitled "I am your friend when no one else is" and found 25,000 friends in a matter of weeks. Jeremy Goeckner and Craig McFarland launched their Peanut Butter and Biscuits podcast. Thea Newcomb, who cofounded Lasso Con, a Ted Lasso-inspired virtual conference, told me: "This show, and our community, gave me such a feeling of connection and belonging."

How to Be a Lioness (Not a Panda) came about because just as Ted inspired me, Rebecca and Keeley did too. Their solidarity as women felt powerful to me. We live in difficult times. The pandemic might have passed, but climate change has not. The Pew Research Center finds that women are more worried about it than men. Oftentimes, it is women who are keeping families together, feeling the burden of domestic duties while also trying to get ahead in their careers. It is easy to feel overwhelmed. Uplifting messages and solidarity with other women like Rebecca and Keeley help.

Jason Sudeikis has said that he liked the Boy Scouts' idea of leaving a campsite cleaner than when you found it. The *Ted Lasso* legacy is just that. He created an uncynical, loving, feminist universe where kindness prevails, where self-belief gets things done and equal respect for fellow humans, regardless of gender, matters. And just as Ted would say, I like that.

ACKNOWLEDGMENTS

A big thank you to Jason Sudeikis and Brendan Hunt for coming up with the idea of Ted Lasso in the first place, and all the writers, cast and crew that brought it to life. We, your fans, appreciate you! Thank you also to the amazing Ted Lasso community, many of whom bought my first Ted Lasso book, and even left me kind reviews. Boy, do I appreciate you! Closer to home, thank you my dear friend Amanda Peppe for your literary brilliance and help, Robyn Foyster for your unwavering support, Darlene Chan, agent-extraordinaire for your enthusiasm, Eilis Flynn for your editing skills, Tom Norland for your design talent, my fabulous husband, David, who is just the best, and all the women I am lucky enough to count as girlfriends.

REFERENCES

Introduction

With Ted Lasso, Hannah Waddingham and Juno Temple's On-and-Off screen Friendship Flips the Sports Comedy Script, by Caroline Framke. Variety. *https://variety.com/2021/tv/features/ted-lasso-season-2-hannah-waddingham-juno-temple-1235019877/*

Hannah Waddingham and Juno Temple on Rebecca and Keeley's Relationship. *https://www.youtube.com/watch?v=wky1vMLlhkI*

Gender Pay Gap in US Hasn't Changed Much in Two Decades, by Carolina Aragao. Pew Research Center. *https://www.pewresearch.org/short-reads/2023/03/01/gender-pay-gap-facts/*

Women Hold a Record Number of Corporate Seats. The bad News: It's Barely over 25 percent and It's Slowing Down, by Alexandra Olson and Associated Press. Fortune. *https://fortune.com/2022/09/30/how-many-women-sit-corporate-boards-record-28-percent-russell-3000/*

Facts and figures: Women's Leadership and Political Participation. UN Women. *https://www.unwomen.org/en/what-we-do/leadership-and-political-participation/facts-and-figures*

Women Continue to Outnumber Men in College Completion, by Jessica Bryant. Best Colleges. *https://www.bestcolleges.com/news/analysis/2021/11/19/women-complete-college-more-than-men/*

Eight Out of Ten Firms Pay Men More Than Women, by Nicu Calcea BBC. *https://www.bbc.com/news/business-65179430*

The Eternal Sunshine of Juno Temple, by Jessica Goldstein. Marie Claire. *https://www.marieclaire.com/culture/a37069344/juno-temple-ted-lasso-interview-2021/*

1 Be a Great Girlfriend

The Tending Instinct: Women, Men and the Biology of Relationships, by Shelley E. Taylor Ph.D (Holt)

The Lifelong Benefits of Strong Female Friendships: Why Female Support is Key, from Career Goals to Healthy living, by Danielle Page. *https://thewell.northwell.edu/womens-health/importance-of-female-friendships#:~:text=Research%20from%20UCLA%20suggests%20that,than%20those%20without%20close%20friendships.*

According to Science Your Girl Squad Can Help You Release More Oxytocin, by Laura Barcella. Healthline. *https://www.healthline.com/health/womens-health/benefits-of-a-girlsquad-and-female-friendships*

Social Networks, Social Support, and Survival After Breast Cancer Diagnosis – Journal of Clinical Oncology. *https://pubmed.ncbi.nlm.nih.gov/16505430/*

Women With More Social Connections Have Better Survival. 2016. Breast Cancer Research News. *https://www.breastcancer.org/research-news/social-connections-linked-to-better-survival*

An Exposure-Wide and Mendelian Randomization Approach to Identifying Modifiable Factors for the Prevention of Depression. Karmel W. Choi. The American Journal of Psychiatry. https://ajp.psychiatryonline.org/doi/10.1176/appi.ajp.2020.19111158

Social Support and the Perception of Geographical Slant – Simone Schnall, University of Plymouth, Kent Harber, Rutgers University at Newark, Jeanine Stefanucci, College of William and Mary, Dennis Proffitt, University of Virginia. *https://www.ncbi.nlm.nih.gov/pmc/articles/PMC3291107/*

Find a girlfriend. *www.girlfriendsocial.com*

2 Be a Mentor

Lean In: Women, Work, and the Will to Lead, by Sheryl Sandberg. (Alfred A Knopf)

Lean In: A Conversation with Sheryl Sandberg and Adam Freed. *https://www.asugsvsummit.com/video/lean-in-a-conversation-with-sheryl-sandberg-and-adam-freed*

Women in the Workplace 2022 Report. McKinsey and Lean In. *https://womenintheworkplace.com*

Women Now Outnumber Men in the US College-Educated Labor Force, by Richard Fry. Pew Research Center. *https://www.pewresearch.org/short-reads/2022/09/26/women-now-outnumber-men-in-the-u-s-college-educated-labor-force/#:~:text=Women%20now%20outnumber%20men%20in%20the%20U.S.%20college%2Deducated%20labor%20force&text=Women%20have%20overtaken%20men%20and,Center%20analysis%20of%20government%20data.*

Women Leaders Make Work Better. Here's the Science Behind How to Promote Them, by Amy Novtney. American Psychological Association. *https://www.apa.org/topics/women-girls/female-leaders-make-work-better#:~:text=Female%20leaders%20demonstrate%20more%20transformational,with%20men%2C%20study%20results%20show.*

Gender and the Evaluation of Leaders: A Meta-Analysis, A.H. Eagly. APA PsycNet. *https://psycnet.apa.org/doiLanding?doi=10.1037%2Famp0000494*

Where Women Work. A Study by The American Psychological Association Reinforces Perception of Women as Equally Competent, If Not More Competent, Than Men in The Workforce. American Psychological Association. *https://www.wherewomenwork.com/Career/1972/American-Psychological-Association-study-women-equally-competent-to-men*

Women Are More Productive at Work than Men, According to New research, by Robby Berman. World Economic Forum. *https://www.weforum.org/agenda/2018/10/women-are-more-productive-than-men-at-work-these-days*

Gender, Expectations and Why Girls Are Outperforming Boys, by Dr. Roger Wilson, Grand Valley State University. *https://scholarworks.gvsu.edu/cgi/viewcontent.cgi?article=1087&context=colleagues*

Boys Left Behind: Education Gender gaps Across the US, by Richard Reeves and Ember Smith. Brookings. *https://www.brookings.edu/articles/boys-left-behind-education-gender-gaps-across-the-us/*

A-level Data Shows Record Grades and Biggest Gender Gap in a Decade, by Pamela Duncan, Ashley Kirk, Cath Levett and Niamh McIntyre. The Guardian. *https://www.theguardian.com/education/2021/aug/10/a-level-results-top-5-data-takeaways*

The Female Quotient, Signature Equity Lounges *https://www.thefemalequotient.com*

Lean In Circles. *https://leanin.org/circles#!*

Albright Alliance *https://www.allbrightalliance.com*

Women Love Tech *https://womenlovetech.com*

Game Changers *https://gamechangers.com.au*

3 Be Ambitious

Strong Woman: Ambition, Grit and a Great Pair of Heels, by Karren Brady (HarperCollins).

Women Working in Football. *https://www.ns-businesshub.com/business/women-in-football-premier-league/*

Dispelling the Myths of the Gender Ambition Gap, by Katie Abouzahr, Matt Krenz, Claire Tracey, and Miki Tusaka BCG. *https://www.bcg.com/publications/2017/people-organization-leadership-change-dispelling-the-myths-of-the-gender-ambition-gap*

Which Sports Teams Have the Most Women in Leadership? *https://www.casino.org/blog/sports-room-diversity/*

4. Be Positive and Empathetic

KPMG 2022 Women Business Leaders Outlook 2022. Women Leaders More People-Focused and Empathetic Than Male Counterparts. *https://www.biznesstransform.com/women-leaders-more-people-focused-and-empathetic-than-male-counterparts-finds-kpmg/#:~:text=Women%20leaders%20 emerged%20as%20significantly,instead%20prioritizing%20buying%20new%20technology.*

The Analysis of 194 Countries, published by the Centre for Economic Policy Research and the World Economic Forum. *https://papers.ssrn.com/sol3/papers.cfm?abstract_id=3617953*

Female-led Countries Handled Coronavirus Better Study Suggests, by Jon Henley. The Guardian. *https://www.theguardian.com/world/2020/aug/18/female-led-countries-handled-coronavirus-better-study-jacinda-ardern-angela-merkel*

If Women Are Better Leaders, Then Why Are They Not in Charge, by Dr. Tomas Premuzic. Forbes. *https://www.forbes.com/sites/tomaspremuzic/2021/03/07/if-women-are-better-leaders-then-why-are-they-not-in-charge/?sh=15016c546c88*

The Business Case for Emotional Intelligence. *http://www.eiconsortium.org/reports/business_case_for_ei.html*

McKinsey and Lean In. Women in the Workplace 2022 Report. *https://womenintheworkplace.com*

5 Be Vulnerable and Think for the Long-term

When Women Lead: What They Achieve, Why they Succeed, How We Can Learn From Them, by Julia Boorstin. (Avid Reader Press)

CNBC's Julia Boorstin Shares What Happens When

Women Lead, by Jessica Abo. Entrepreneur. *https://www.entrepreneur.com/leadership/cnbcs-julia-boorstin-shares-what-happens-when-women-lead/440779*

Women Score Higher Than Men in Most Leadership Skills, by Jack Zenger and Joseph Folman. Harvard Business Review: *https://hbr.org/2019/06/research-women-score-higher-than-men-in-most-leadership-skills#:~:text=As%20people%20age%20their%20confidence,hand%2C%20gain%2029%20percentile%20points.*

Four Reasons Intuition is an Essential Leadership Skill, Laura Stupple. Entrepreneur. *https://www.entrepreneur.com/leadership/4-reasons-intuition-is-an-essential-leadership-skill/426726#:~:text=Leading%20with%20intuition%20makes%20you,intuition%20complements%20the%20hard%20evidence.*

The Power of Vulnerability, by Brené Brown. www.brenebrown.com

6 Be Resilient

Rethink What You Know About High Achieving Women, by Robin Ely, Pamela Stone, Colleen Ammerman. Harvard Business Review. *https://hbr.org/2014/12/rethink-what-you-know-about-high-achieving-women*

Women@ Work 2023 Deloitte. *https://www.deloitte.*

com/global/en/issues/work/content/women-at-work-global-outlook.html

Why Women Startups Are a Better Bet. BCG *https://www.bcg.com/publications/2018/why-women-owned-startups-are-better-bet*

Twice As Likely to Be Asked to Make Tea or About Their Kids, Than Men. Samsung Business 2022. *https://news.samsung.com/uk/gender-bias-in-the-workplace-women-more-than-twice-as-likely-to-be-asked-to-make-tea-or-about-their-kids-than-men#:~:text=The%20latest%20research%20from%20Samsung,is%20showing%20up%20at%20work.*

Women Led Startups Received Just 2.3 percent of VC Funding in 2020, by Ashley Bittner and Brigette Lau. Harvard Business Review. *https://hbr.org/2021/02/women-led-startups-received-just-2-3-of-vc-funding-in-2020*

When Women Lead: What They Achieve, Why they Succeed, How We Can Learn From Them, by Julia Boorstin. (Avid Reader Press)

Shine Theory, by Aminatou Sow and Ann Friedman. *https://www.shinetheory.com*

7 Move the Goalposts

The Gender Divide That Fails Football's Bottom Line: The Commercial Case for Gender Equality. Fairgame 2022. *https://static1.squarespace.com/*

static/6047aabc7130e94a70ed3515/t/6225fcd351 786a64ba4421b0/1646656733257/The+Gender+ Divide+That+Fails+Football%27s+Bottom+Line+- +Fair+Game+Report+March+2022.pdf

Lionesses: How Football Came Home. (Adhoc Films. Altitude Film Entertainment). Amazon Prime Video.

Soccer Pioneers Recall the First Women's World Cup, by Claire Wolters. National Geographic. *https://www.nationalgeographic.com/culture/article/ soccer-pioneers-recall-first-womens-world-cup*

The History of Women's Football in the UK, by Eleanor Dickens. British Library. *https://www.bl.uk/womens-rights/articles/ the-history-of-womens-football-in-the-uk*

Unsuitable for Females and Should Not Be Encouraged, By Chrissie Goldrick. Australian Geographic. *https://www.australiangeographic. com.au/topics/history-culture/2023/07/ unsuitable-for-females-and-should-not-be-encouraged/*

Female Soccer Players Earn 25 Cents to the Dollar of Men at World Cup. CNN. *https://www.cnn. com/2023/07/20/football/womens-world-cup-pay- prize-money-spt-intl-dg/index.html*

Ted Lasso Star Hannah Waddingham Wants Fans to Watch Women's Sports. *https://www.usatoday.com/ story/sports/soccer/2023/07/14/hannah-waddingham- ted-lasso-fans-watch-womens-sports/70399239007/*

8 Believe in You

The Confidence Gap in Men and Women: Why It Matters and How to Overcome It. *https://www.forbes.com/sites/jackzenger/2018/04/08/the-confidence-gap-in-men-and-women-why-it-matters-and-how-to-overcome-it/?sh=64432e703bfa*

The Confidence Gap, by Katty Kay and Claire Shipman. The Atlantic. *https://www.theatlantic.com/magazine/archive/2014/05/the-confidence-gap/359815/*

Seventy-five Percent of Women Experience Imposter Syndrome in the Workplace, by Luciana Paulise. Forbes. *https://www.forbes.com/sites/lucianapaulise/2023/03/08/75-of-women-executives-experience-imposter-syndrome-in-the-workplace/?sh=5e0f29cd6899*

KPMG study finds 75 percent of female executives across industries have experienced imposter syndrome in their careers. *https://info.kpmg.us/news-perspectives/people-culture/kpmg-study-finds-most-female-executives-experience-imposter-syndrome.html*

Female and Younger Leaders More Susceptible to Imposter Syndrome, by Rachel Muller-Heyndyk. HR Magazine. *https://www.hrmagazine.co.uk/content/news/female-and-younger-leaders-more-susceptible-to-imposter-syndrome/*

Michelle Obama on Leadership, Balance, and Battling

Imposter Syndrome, by Melissa Twigg. Tatler Asia. *https://www.tatlerasia.com/gen-t/leadership/ap-six-lessons-we-learnt-from-michelle-obama*

You Are a Badass: How to Stop Doubting your Greatness and Start Living an Awesome Life, by Jen Sincero. (Hodder & Stoughton)

The Confidence Code: The Science and Art of Self-Assurance – What Women Should Know, by Katty Kay and Claire Shipman. (HarperCollins)

9 Be True to You

Hannah Waddingham Sounds Off on Women being Pitted Against Each other, by Alyssa Ray. Eonline. *https://www.eonline.com/news/1290818/ted-lassos-hannah-waddingham-sounds-off-on-women-being-pitted-against-each-other*

A Conversation with Hannah Waddingham and Juno Temple *https://www.youtube.com/watch?v=nR1wBfv0Mis&t=366s*

Juno Temple Interview, by Max Gao. Harper's Bazaar. *https://www.harpersbazaar.com/culture/film-tv/a43298655/juno-temple-ted-lasso-season-3-intervew/*

Hannah Waddingham on The View. *https://www.youtube.com/watch?v=J5etO05OxQs&t=330s*

Hannah Waddingham, interview in You Magazine. Daily Mail. *https://www.dailymail.co.uk/femail/article-11887021/*

Hannah-Waddinghams-Emmy-winning-role-global-hit-Ted-Lasso-ignited-screen-career.html

Hannah Waddingham and Juno Temple on Their Game-changing Friendship. Variety. *https://www.youtube.com/watch?v=oB2_Igl6M-I*

Juno Temple on her Character in Comedy Debut Ted Lasso: Keeley has Saved my Mental Health, Truly. By Joe Utichi. Deadline. *https://deadline.com/2021/06/juno-temple-ted-lasso-interview-apple-tv-emmy-1234770057/*

Women are Advancing in the Workplace but Women of Color Lag Behind. Brookings. *https://www.brookings.edu/people/adia-harvey-wingfield/*

Sarah Niles Needed Ted Lasso Too, by Christopher Orr. New York Times *https://www.nytimes.com/2021/07/30/arts/television/ted-lasso-sarah-niles.html*

Ted Lasso's Sarah Niles on Why Sharon is More Than Just an Anti-Ted, by Jack King. Vulture. *https://www.vulture.com/article/ted-lasso-sarah-niles-sharon-season-two-interview.html*

Black Representation in TV and Film. McKinsey. *https://www.mckinsey.com/featured-insights/diversity-and-inclusion/black-representation-in-film-and-tv-the-challenges-and-impact-of-increasing-diversity#*

You've Got to Bask in the Sun of Life, Sarah Niles on her Newfound Acclaim, by Michael Hogan.

The Guardian. *https://www.theguardian.com/tv-and-radio/2022/aug/21/youve-got-to-bask-in-the-sun-of-life-actor-sarah-niles-on-her-newfound-acclaim*

10 Be Kind

Why Sexual Harassment Programs Backfire, by Frank Dobbin and Alexandra Kalev. Harvard Business Review *https://hbr.org/2020/05/why-sexual-harassment-programs-backfire*

What About Men? By Caitlin Moran. (Ebury Press)

Men and Depression, by Fredric Rabinowitz, Ph.D., American Psychological Association, Guidelines for Practice with Men and Boys. *www.apa.org*

Suicide Statistics. Center for Disease Control and Prevention (CDC) *https://www.cdc.gov/suicide/suicide-data-statistics.html*

Why More Men than Women Die by Suicide, by Helene Schumacher. BBC. *https://www.bbc.com/future/article/20190313-why-more-men-kill-themselves-than-women*

An Investigation of Masculinity Attitudes, Gender, and Attitudes Towards Psychological Help, by Omar Yousaf. APA PsycNet (American Psychological Association) *https://psycnet.apa.org/record/2014-12450-001*

Author's Note

Man's Search for Meaning, by Viktor E Frankl (Beacon Press)

What Would Ted Lasso Do? How Ted's Positive Approach Can Help You, by Lucy Broadbent. (Uncommon Publishing).

Ted Lasso Tours *https://www.tedlassotour.com*

Coach Beard's Book Group. *https://coachbeardsbookclub.*

podbean.com

Jason Sudiekis Interview, by Tim Lewis. The Guardian

https://www.theguardian.com/tv-and-radio/2023/may/14/jason-sudeikis-interview-ted-lasso

If you enjoyed this book, please consider leaving a review on Amazon. Authors survive by their reviews. I appreciate you! This QR code will take you straight there.

ALSO BY AMAZON BEST SELLING AUTHOR LUCY BROADBENT

What Would Ted Lasso Do?
How Ted's Positive Approach Can Help You

Need a little inspiration? Discover how Ted Lasso's "Believe" sign can motivate you in your own life, how you can learn to be optimistic and resilient like Ted, and how his core beliefs could even help you live longer. Winner of 2022 Indie Book of The Year Award, this best-selling, easy-to-read guide reveals the psychology behind Ted's life lessons. It's like having Ted Lasso as your very own life coach.

Ted's heart-warming philosophies are rooted in the positive psychology movement and take audiences into the world of self-help, sometimes unknowingly. Remember when Ted told Sam to 'Be a goldfish' because it has a short memory. Confucius bequeathed his own version: “To be wronged is nothing, unless you continue to remember it.”

Through plausibly real and difficult situations on the TV show, we see how Ted turns negatives into positives, adversity into acceptance, selfish behavior into self-aware behavior. He ensures we understand that it is how we react to difficult situations that can make a difference between coming out smiling or not.

Mixing TV fandom with psychology, celebrity journalist Lucy Broadbent unearths the wisdom behind Ted’s life lessons, explaining its value and offering tricks to help all of us lead happier, healthier, kinder lives, the *Ted Lasso* way.

Printed in Great Britain
by Amazon